DARK PERIL

THE DEPARTMENT Z SERIES

Dark Peril

Department Z

John Creasey

OPEN ROAD
INTEGRATED MEDIA
NEW YORK

Copyright © 1944 by John Creasey

ISBN: 978-1-5040-9271-5

This edition published in 2024 by Open Road Integrated Media, Inc.
180 Maiden Lane
New York, NY 10038
www.openroadmedia.com

DARK PERIL

1

THE MEN WHO COULD NOT SEE

The round-shouldered man sitting at the large, littered desk, drew in his breath and pushed his chair back. The electric lamp, immediately above his head, reflected from his bald pate and cast the shadows of his bushy eyebrows on a sheet of paper covered with figures. Except for his heavy breathing, the large, book-lined room was very quiet, but now and again a howl of wind outside disturbed the silence.

The man closed his eyes. He sat like that for fully five minutes, then opened them and leaned forward, looking down at the paper. The rows of figures remained clear for only a few seconds; they gradually merged into one another, and he could not read them. He stood up abruptly, with his hands clenched.

"I can't go on like this!" he muttered, "it's fantastic. I can't even *see!*"

He took off his glasses and rubbed his watery eyes. They were painful and red-rimmed. He went out of the room and walked along the dimly-lighted passage, but before he reached the landing he blundered into the wall, and stopped short.

"It *can't* be as bad as that!" he said aloud.

He replaced his glasses, and peered ahead of him. At first, the richly-carved balustrade along the landing showed clearly, but gradually the dark line thickened and moved until it merged with the oak panelling of the wall behind. He stood quite still, with his lips parted and one hand stretched out, as if to fend off some evil thing.

A door opened downstairs.

He heard voices, and the light laughter of a girl, yet they hardly registered on his mind. He did not move as the voices drew nearer and footsteps sounded on the stairs. A deep voice alternated with the girl's.

"I'm not a bit sure that I ought to worry him now."

"Oh, Daddy won't mind," said Julia Hartley, confidently. "Don't be put off by his forbidding manner, Mike, and don't be offended if he suddenly looks away from you and starts scribbling: I don't think he really cares tuppence about anything but his work."

"A pillar of reconstruction," said the man called Mike.

"*Daddy!*" gasped the girl.

Sir Basil Hartley had not understood the conversation, and had not realised that they had reached the landing. He had not moved from the moment the wooden balustrade had become part of the background. At the girl's exclamation, he started and looked towards the sound, and he could vaguely discern the shapes of his daughter and her companion.

"Daddy, what on earth—"

"It's—it's nothing, my dear, nothing," muttered Hartley. "I have a severe headache, and I must go and rest." He turned abruptly—and walked straight into the wall. He reeled back and put his hand to his forehead, his whole body trembling. "I—I have been overworking," he went on. "My eyes have given out, but a night's sleep will put them right. Lead—lead me to my room, Julia, will you, please."

The girl went forward and took his arm, then shot a glance at her companion, a tall, good-looking man, who was dressed in a well-cut suit of light grey. His hair, a little untidy, was inclined to curl.

"I'll see you in a few minutes," she said.

"All right," said Mike Errol, quietly, "but you ought to send for a doctor. Your father mustn't take risks with his eyesight." He was looking oddly at Hartley, frowning and paying little attention to Julia. She was as tall as her father, and her dark, wavy hair showed up against Hartley's baldness. "Can I telephone for you?"

"Do you really think it's necessary?" asked Julia, dubiously.

"No, there is no need to send for Lewis," said Hartley, sharply; "it is just that I have been overdoing it. Perhaps—perhaps if you will make a solution of boracic acid powder and tepid water, Julia. I will bathe my eyes."

"Yes, of course," said Julia. "Oh, Mike, would you mind going into the bathroom, and—"

She had started to speak while looking at her father, but now she turned her head, and saw Mike Errol walking down the stairs. She opened her mouth to call him back, but changed her mind. She led her father to his bedroom, which was next to his study, and, when he was sitting back in an easy chair, she went to the bathroom and opened the first-aid box and the medicine cabinet. She took out what she wanted, and hurried downstairs. There was no sign of Mike Errol, and she went to the kitchen to put on a kettle.

"I hope he *isn't* telephoning for Lewis," she said, uneasily.

Mike Errol was at the telephone; he had just replaced the receiver, after putting in a call to a Whitehall number. He stood with one hand in his pocket and a cigarette jutting from his lips, frowning towards the door.

Lyddon House, on the outskirts of Woking, was large enough to need a staff of three or four. Only one old servant, the house-keeper, remained, and she was out for the evening. Julia Hartley had prepared dinner, taken a tray up to her father, and had enjoyed having her meal with Mike Errol, a comparatively new acquaintance who both appealed to and puzzled her. It had been an unconventional evening and Mike had sprung another surprise when he had said that he would very much like to ask her father one or two questions. He had been vague, but he had a way with him, and she had assured him that her father would not object.

There was a brief delay on the Whitehall call. As Julia walked along the hall, with the small glass of boracic acid solution in her hand, the telephone bell rang. She heard Mike answer it, and went straight to the drawing-room, which was long, narrow, and furnished in neo-Jacobean style.

"You aren't telephoning the doctor, are you?"

"Oh, no," said Mike, with an engaging smile. "Orders are orders! I forgot a call I should have made earlier, and I didn't think I need worry to ask you just now. Do you mind?"

"No, of course not."

"Can I help?"

"No, I shall be all right," she said, and hurried out.

Mike Errol's smile faded as he spoke into the mouthpiece again, and he did a curious thing. He spelt his surname, backwards, very quickly. Gordon Craigie, the man at the other end, did not seem to find this peculiar, for he said:

"Yes, go on, Mike."

"It's happened again," said Mike Errol, in a voice which was barely audible two yards away from him. "I didn't have a chance to see Hartley before it was too late. My fault, I'm afraid, I didn't expect anything to happen so quickly. The symptoms are the same, as far as I can tell. I met him a few minutes ago. He was as blind as a bat, and looked as if he had just discovered it. What's my best move?"

"Have you sent for a doctor?"

"Hartley rejected the idea at once. He doesn't want to admit that it's anything serious. I don't know either him or Julia Hartley well enough to show the iron hand, unless you think it's worth causing offence."

"Stay there and do whatever you think best until Faversham arrives," said Craigie. "I'll get him to come over at once. You'll have to handle the situation as best you can, Mike—sorry."

"No need to be sorry," said Mike Errol. "Right-ho, old chap. I'll get well dug in. Shall I say I've sent for Faversham?"

"There's no reason why you shouldn't."

"May Hartley know that it's not the first time such a thing has happened?"

"It won't surprise me if he knows about the other cases," said Gordon Craigie. "I give you a free hand, Mike. I must go, a bell's ringing."

Craigie rang off and Mike Errol replaced his receiver, then shrugged his wide shoulders and stubbed out his cigarette. Julia Hartley was an unpredictable young woman who might resent any high-handed action on his part; his best plan would be to tell her a little of what he knew, and thus justify himself. Even after that she might accuse him of trying to worm his way into her confidence on a false pretext, and might not be appeased. He was thoughtful as he went into the hall, in time to hear her calling from the head of the stairs.

"Mike!"

"Can I help?" He hurried up, taking the stairs two at a time.

"Yes—would you mind helping him into bed? He really can't manage, and he doesn't want me to help him. I—I hate asking you."

Mike smiled and squeezed her arm before hurrying along to Hartley's room. The old man was sitting in his shirt-sleeves and struggling to unfasten his shoe-laces. A surgical eye glass and a piece of cotton-wool were on a bedside table.

"Let me give you a hand," said Mike, cheerfully.

"There is no need—" Hartley began, but his protest faded.

Five minutes later he was in bed, with his eyes closed. Mike put out the main light, but left on a subdued bedside tablelamp, and went out. He closed the door softly. Julia was not in sight, and he stepped across to the bathroom, and looked through the medical cabinet swiftly. He took out a small, blue bottle bearing the label: "*Eye Lotion—For Tired Eyes.*" For a moment he hesitated, then he slipped the bottle into his pocket, and went out.

Julia was coming up the stairs, carrying a tray with a glass of milk; steam was rising from it. Mike said: "That's a good thought," and opened the door for her, but he did not go into the bedroom again. Instead, he waited near the open door of the study until she came out with the empty glass. Her fine grey eyes were narrowed, and her full lips set.

"I'm beginning to think we *ought* to send for Dr. Lewis," she said. "Daddy seems absolutely exhausted. I told him a hundred times that unless he rested much more than he did, he would crack up."

"If he'd rested for a month it wouldn't have helped him," Mike said.

"It wouldn't have—" she broke off, frowning. "What do you mean? What are you making a mystery about?"

She was a striking-looking woman when she was frowning, and a creature of contrasts, for in her light moods she was almost kittenish. There were people who said that her father had thoroughly spoiled her, and that he had been wrong not to allow a relative to bring her up, after her mother had died when she was four—twenty years before. Instead, Hartley had employed a woman who was partly a foster-mother and partly governess, and had kept the reins of control himself. She had a wide face, a fine complexion, and a short nose, which was quite straight. None of her features was particularly good, but the general effect was pleasing.

Some said that she was headstrong; Mike, who had known her for a little less than a week, agreed. She was also generous to a fault, often impulsively so, and he did not think it wrong that she held some strong opinions.

"Will you please explain?" she demanded.

Mike grinned.

"Not while you're fixing me with the evil eye!"

In spite of herself, she smiled.

"Mike, what *are* you driving at?"

"Well, it's like this," he said, lightly. "I am not soldier, sailor nor airman, as you perceive, but I have a job to do, and in my humble way I do it as best I can. Often it sends me to strange places, and often it gives me work which is distasteful. I didn't *like* pretending that I was only attracted by the glow in your eyes when we met at Chubby Foster's, but I had to pretend that was so. Actually I wanted to meet you because you are who you are—daughter of Sir Basil Hartley. My mission was purely protective. It's failed, horribly. You see, three other men, working along similar lines to him, have been suddenly afflicted by blindness."

She took the shock well. Her hands clenched and her head lifted a little, thrusting her square chin forward.

"I see," she said slowly. "So you expected this to happen?"

"I didn't so much expect it as feel afraid that it might," said Mike. "I was detailed to try to find out whether there was any suggestion of eye trouble with your father. How long has he used that eye lotion?"

"For years. I—what do you mean?"

"In at least two cases the trouble was caused by an irritant put into an eye-lotion which was in daily use," said Mike, "and the same thing might have happened again. Julia, don't ask me dozens of questions, because I don't know the answers. I'm only doing my little bit in the work of finding out what is behind it. I think you'll have to take it for granted that the trouble with your father's eyes is not the result of overstrain, but has been deliberately contrived."

"Are you suggesting that someone has tampered with the lotion?" demanded Julia.

"It's possible. I've the bottle here, and I'll have it examined," said Mike, taking the bottle out of his pocket to show her, and then putting it back. "It's not easy to advise this course or that, and I know you must be feeling pretty worked up. Actually, I've gone further than I should have done in saying so much. You'll keep it to yourself, won't you?"

"I see no reason why I should," she said, coldly. "I don't even know that you are telling the truth. You may pretend to be working under orders for some Government department—that is what you're implying, I suppose?—but actually you may be doing nothing of the kind."

"I can't complain about that reasoning," admitted Mike. "Let's put it this way: will you keep quiet until I've had the chance of proving that I'm on the square—say, until tomorrow mid-day? That isn't asking too much, is it?"

"I suppose not," she conceded, "but I can't admit that you were justified in tricking me. Nothing you say will alter the fact that I resent it very much. You should have come to me and told me what you suspected, and I would have done everything I could to help."

Mike grinned.

"You would probably have told me that I was talking nonsense, and shown me the door! You would certainly have told your father and worried him when worry might not have been necessary. The main point is that I acted under orders." He stood up, and rested a hand lightly on her arm. "Julia, I've come to know you fairly well. I know now that you're quite trustworthy, but I didn't a week ago, and I might not be able to convince everyone concerned. They're a cynical, hard-bitten crowd, who take a lot of convincing. Yes," he added, squeezing her arm gently, in spite of her growing anger, "they *will* think it possible that you doped the eye lotion! Until, of course, we've convinced them to the contrary."

"I have never heard anything so ridiculous!" stormed Julia, wrenching her arm away.

She broke off abruptly, for downstairs there was a bump, followed by a muttered imprecation, then silence as Mike stepped swiftly to the door.

2

THE LIGHT-HEARTED COUSIN

Softly though he moved, Mike Errol knew that if whoever was downstairs had his wits about him, he would know that someone was approaching. The light from the study cast Mike's shadow on the wall of the passage, and it was evident until he was half-way to the landing. The wide staircase and the narrow, L-shaped hall beneath were richly carpeted; he made no sound, but before he could look into the hall a man began to sing.

"I'm Dreaming of a White—chriss-mas! I'm dream—hic!" He broke off, and there was the sound of a chair falling. "Dam' thing!" muttered the newcomer, crossly, "couldn't it see me coming? *Shh!* Don't let Uncle know I'm back!"

Mike stood at the head of the stairs and surveyed the man in the hall. He was young, and his red hair was untidy. He looked slim and not bad-looking, although the angle at which Mike saw him was an odd one. He was standing and swaying back on his heels, with a finger at his lips as he regarded a William and Mary chair which lay on its side. Above it was a painting of a man in Victorian garb; the eyes glared down on him, as if in disapproval.

"Fergus!" exclaimed Julia, from Mike's side. Her voice must have carried to the man in the hall. "And he's—"

The young man looked up and waved his hand wildly, shaking his head at the same time, to enjoin silence. He took two steps forward, and nearly fell. Julia pushed past Mike and hurried down the stairs, reaching the foot as her cousin—a relationship of which Mike soon learned—put a foot on the bottom stair.

"Are you *quite* mad?" demanded Julia, angrily.

"*Ssshhh!* Don't tell Uncle—yet!" The young man peered into her eyes, then rested a hand on her shoulder. "Be on my side, Julia. Always were a good shport—be on my side? Hic!" He grinned. "I'm not drunk, s'fact. I'm not drunk. Just—just a little gay, that's all. Gay—light-hearted! That's me!" He hiccoughed again, and added: "Is he still up? What's his temper like tonight? Had—had to return, to inshi—in*sist*—on my rights. Abshutely!" Fergus Grey swayed backwards again as he patted Julia's cheek; then he looked up the stairs and went rigid. He raised a hand slowly and pointed towards Mike, who was coming down. "Who-whossat?" he demanded, with drunken annoyance. "Didn't know—third party—present. Shay, *Julia.* What—what have *you* been up to? Heeby-jeeby! Uncle's out, and you—oh-ho-ho-ho! *Now* I've got something on you, my pretty lass, now you'll be on my shi-ide, or—*hic!*"

Julia slapped his face.

Mike was just behind her, and could not see her expression, but he saw the amazement on the newcomer's face as the blow landed. Grey went back and sat down on the floor, causing a loud thud.

"Oh, *Jew*-lia! You—you hit me!" He looked up at Mike and gulped. "You saw her! You're a witness. Assault, that's what it is. Assault. Deliberate. Just because—just because I twigged her little game! Aw right, just you wait until I see Uncle. An' I'm gonna see him! I'm going—I'm going—I'm going to sit right here until he comes. You can't move me. Impossible. I'm here until he comes. *Un-cull!*" He raised his voice until it sounded like a view halloo. "*Un-cuuuuul!*"

"If you don't—" began Julia.

"All right," said Mike. He passed her, bent down and yanked the startled young man to his feet, and hoisted him over his shoulder, as if he were handling a laden sack. He carried him into the drawing-room and dumped him unceremoniously on to a settee. The young man bounced up and down, his mouth gaping; he did not seem to have the breath to protest.

Mike turned to Julia.

"I don't think you want your father disturbed, do you?"

"Of course not." Julia was looking at her cousin, with her face set. "You have my permission to throw Fergus out of the house. The only trouble is"—her voice broke a little—"you'll never be able to keep him out."

"S'right," chimed in the young man. "No right to—to keep me out. No right. Have the law on you if you try. Fact. And—" he stared wide-eyed at Mike, and formed his words with great precision. "I don't like your young man. Unpleasant young man. No brains. All brawn. Scram, sir!"

"No scram," said Mike.

"No scram?"

"No."

"Please yourself," said the young man, sitting up and getting unsteadily to his feet, "Shir, I apologise. Most discourteous. We haven't been introduced. Julia, I inshist—introduce us. After all, it's not right. To be carried about by a man you don't know. Not right at all. Is it, sir?" He appealed earnestly to Mike.

Julia spoke wearily.

"Mike, this is my cousin, Fergus Grey. Mike Errol." She raised her hands. "Fergus, why won't you be sensible? You know it only leads to trouble when you come here, and to come in drunk like this is—is just asking for a real quarrel. You're lucky that Daddy's had a bilious attack and is lying down. Go away, there's a good fellow."

"Certainly not," said Grey, clearly. "Here I am, and here I stay. Mike, old boy—back me up, will you? You look a friendly cove. Sensible fellow, I should think. *Can* anyone throw me out of my own house? I ask you—a simple matter of—of—well, you know what I mean? Is it right, that's all I ask you to say, I'll take your word for it. If it's right, I'll go out and *never* come back!"

"It isn't your house!" Julia said, sharply, but she shot a quick embarrassed glance at Mike.

"It *ought* to be," flashed Grey. "I think—"

"I think you ought to know that, unless you stop this drivel, I shall pick you up and throw you out," Mike said. "And, judging from your clothes, it's raining."

"It's nearly stopped," declared Grey, owlishly. "I inspected the weather before I came in. Nearly stopped. I wish—"

He broke off, and his head dropped on his chest. In a few seconds, he was snoring loudly.

"Of all the pigs!" exclaimed Julia. "Mike, I'm dreadfully sorry."

"Don't be sorry," smiled Mike. "Is there a nice, comfortable room where he can sleep it off?"

"Yes."

"I'll carry him," said Mike.

He lifted Grey without any effort and carried him in Julia's wake. She led the way up the stairs, along a passage leading to the right, and into the end room. It was a well-furnished bedroom, with two arm-chairs and two small bookcases by the fireplace. Mike dropped him on the bed, took off his shoes, loosened his collar, and threw an eiderdown over him. All this time, Julia watched him. When he finished, he turned and led her out. At the door he took the key from the lock on the inside and locked the door from the outside, then dropped the key into his pocket.

"Why did you do that?" Julia asked.

"In case he breaks out and goes storming into your father's room," said Mike, lightly. "We don't want that. By the way, I ought to warn you—there will be another visitor soon, a Dr.

Faversham, an oculist of some repute. I'll guarantee that he will arrive sober!"

Julia said: "When did you send for him? I—oh! That's who you were telephoning. You believe in taking things into your own hands, don't you?" she added, sharply.

Mike smiled. "Isn't it helpful, sometimes? After all, I've put two men to bed, and—"

"Please!" She led the way along to the study again, and sat down in her father's chair, pushing away the papers on which he had been working so hard. Then she swung the swivel chair round so that she could look at Mike. "I know you have had a most unpleasant evening. I'm sorry. As I said before, none of it need have happened if you had told me in the first place. As for this eye-specialist, whoever he is, I don't suppose Father will allow him to examine him."

"You'll be wise to persuade him to," said Mike, "because it might make the difference between temporary and total blindness." Seeing her expression, he added quickly: "Obviously it's a possibility that we ought to try to guard against."

She stood up abruptly. "Mike, do you think it will last? Won't he recover his sight? If he's going to be blind, it will kill him!"

Mike shook his head.

"It wouldn't do anything of the kind, and you know it. It would be a blow, but he would find a way of working in spite of the handicap. In any case, it's probably only temporary. Julia, if I seem to probe, forgive me, but—your cousin is rather a queer stick, isn't he?"

"Yes," she said. "I suppose I owe you some kind of an explanation although it's really no business of yours. He—well you've seen what he is. He is seldom really sober. He used to live with us. His father— my father's elder brother—once owned this house, but he and Fergus quarrelled bitterly, and Fergus didn't get a penny more than the law demanded. This house was left to Father. Fergus expected to have it, and to him it remained his home, but a few weeks ago he and Father had a furious quarrel and Fergus went off, vowing he wouldn't come back. Father told him that if he tried to, he would be thrown out." She drew her hand across her forehead, but there was a sharp note in her voice when she added: "Is there any more dirty linen you would like washed?"

"No, come!" protested Mike. "That's not fair."

"Perhaps you think *you've* been fair?"

"I think that it was worth deceiving you to try to prevent an attack of blindness," said Mike, "but if you would rather have the whole affair turned over to the police, I don't mind. They'll be discreet, of course, but a certain amount of publicity will be unavoidable." He spoke brusquely, and his expression was cold. "You've only to say the word."

"Why should the police be called in?" She was obviously startled.

"It could be construed into an attempt to cause your father serious bodily harm," said Mike. "In fact, there wouldn't be a lot of construing necessary! I think I can get permission to handle it on my own, or with my own friends, but that's up to you." He took out his case; she took a cigarette absently, and accepted a light. As she blew out the smoke she stared at him, and spoke quietly.

"You know that I would hate to have the police here."

"Good! Will you also let bygones be bygones, and help me as much as you can?"

"Yes," said Julia, after a moment's hesitation.

"Better!" cried Mike, and grinned. "I didn't think we were made to quarrel!"

Ten minutes afterwards, a ring at the front door heralded the arrival of Dr. Faversham, a small, dark man of few words. He nodded briefly to Mike, bowed distantly to Julia when Mike introduced her, and said that he would have to be quick, as he was due back in London by half-past eleven.

It was then ten o'clock.

In spite of his words, Faversham spent a long time with Hartley, who raised no protest on being told why he had come. The old man now seemed resigned to the situation; that was a curious development, which made Mike thoughtful. Julia stayed in the room with the doctor, and Mike took the opportunity to look through the papers on Hartley's desk.

They meant nothing to him.

The figures and formulæ written in Hartley's neat hand concerned plans for social reforms of various natures, and were more directly concerned with costs. Hartley was an economist who had been on the Advisory Panel to the Government for some time. His knowledge was practically unrivalled, and he had many warm supporters and many admirers. Mike did not know exactly what work he was employed on at that time. It was not his business to know, but it was his business to find out who had brought about the blindness.

After a quarter of an hour he went along to Grey's room, and unlocked it. As he opened the door, he thought he heard a movement, but when he switched on the light Grey was lying with his mouth open and snoring; the eiderdown was over him. Mike went out and locked the door again. He walked heavily away from the room, then returned to it, softly.

The snoring had stopped.

He went down on one knee, and peeped through the keyhole. He saw Grey moving stealthily from the bed. He stood up, smiling with satisfaction, and tip-toed to the landing. From there he watched the door; he could also see along to Hartley's room, from which there came a mutter of voices.

Mike was nothing like so interested in them as he was in Grey's remarkable behaviour. Five minutes passed, and he saw nothing. Then the door which he had locked began to open. Mike slipped back, out of sight, into another room, and watched the landing from there. He saw Grey approach and start to go furtively down the stairs. Grey kept looking over his shoulder, but when he reached the hall he seemed more assured, and he opened the front door and let himself out.

"Now I wonder whether I ought to have stopped him," mused Mike, "or whether Gordon has him watched?"

3

THE CAREFULNESS OF GORDON CRAIGIE

Gordon Craigie, a prematurely-greying, sparsely-built man with craggy, saturnine features and the alert, hooded-lid eyes of an eagle, was well known only to a select few in Whitehall. Many more, as familiar with his slightly stooping figure as with the eccentrically-large-bowled meerschaum he always sported, would have been surprised to learn that he headed a special branch of the secret service—"Department Z," to the initiated—concerned for the most part with counter-espionage. On the night in question, Craigie replaced the receiver, after taking a call from a telephone kiosk in Esher, and looked across the large room in Whitehall to the big man who was seated in an easy-chair before a small coal fire. The big man was William Loftus, Craigie's second-in-command.

Loftus framed a word.

"Who?"

"That was Mark," said Craigie. "He followed Fergus Grey to the Hartley house, where Grey stayed for over an hour, and then followed him to his hotel nearby. He seems to have settled down there for the night. We might get something from Mike before the night's out," he added, "and Faversham's there—Mark saw him arrive. Mike's working inside, as you know."

"So we shall also hear from Faversham," said Loftus, whose large features looked heavy in repose—some said, looked wooden—and who had become very fat since he had taken up his "staff job" with Craigie. He knew the Errol cousins, Mike and Mark, very well. "Not that we need worry about Faversham's report; it's certainly the same business. Four of 'em now. What are we going to do about it?"

"Report," said Craigie, briefly.

Loftus snorted. "A fat lot of good that will do, with the P.M. away. Do you know, Gordon, I doubt whether it has struck any other individual as being remarkable that four such men should have suddenly lost their sight. Overwork—eyestrain—any explanation will satisfy them. To read anything sinister into it is to invite their hearty laughter."

Craigie smiled. "It isn't quite as bad as that."

"It's not far short," grumbled Loftus. "There are times when I despair of the Whitehall mind."

"I don't think you need, Bill," said Craigie, judicially. "We won't go to sleep again. Anyhow, you're wrong in one respect. The P.M. came back last night. I left a note for him at Number 10, and I expect he'll give me a ring before long—so the report won't be neglected!"

Loftus looked startled.

"Back, is he? The foxy blighter! I don't think even the Press knew about it."

"You mean, you didn't," smiled Craigie.

Not long afterwards, Craigie was summoned by telephone to see the Rt. Hon. Graham Hershall, Prime Minister of Great Britain, and by that time he had finished the notes for his report.

It said, briefly, that as three men prominent in the Government's economic plans had become blind by some mysterious means which puzzled doctors, he had arranged that the seven others, who worked on the same Committee as the three afflicted, should be watched; and that one of these men, Sir Basil Hartley, had now become a victim. He did not go into further details, for they could be given when he saw the P.M.; he had little doubt that his precautions would be approved.

He left Loftus in the office, and Loftus went stiffly to his desk and sat down, so that he could answer any telephone calls more conveniently. He had lost a leg in an affair which had nearly cost the Department his services, and he declared to all and sundry that he grew fat because he could not take sufficient exercise.

He wondered how Mike Errol was getting on, for he was acquainted with Julia Hartley, and had himself introduced Mike to her.

At Woking, Dr. Faversham was non-committal, promised to send a lotion along first thing in the morning, and left the house just before eleven o'clock. By then the housekeeper had returned and Julia had told her what had happened. She was a bustling, mannish woman named McFarlane, and she quickly assumed control of the sick-room. Mike and Julia returned to the study.

"I suppose we ought to see how Fergus is getting on," Julia said, restlessly. "And you won't get a train back to-night, Mike—oh, what a business it all is!"

Mike smiled. "A settee will do nicely for me."

"So you've already made up your mind to stay the night," said Julia, rather tartly.

"I counted on it, because there are more curious things than you know of, Julia," admitted Mike. "Fergus is one of them. He wasn't drunk, you know."

"He wasn't—*what?*"

"Drunk. Inebriated. The worse for drink. It was a pretty fair act," Mike admitted. "Has he ever been on the stage?"

"You're talking nonsense!"

"There was a damp patch on his collar and his chest," said Mike, "and the smell of whisky came from there—not his lips. He pronounced some words far too well for a drunk, and made a hash of simple ones which the well-oiled usually pronounce perfectly. Also, when I went up to have a look at him, he started snoring when he heard me at the door, and stopped when he thought I was out of earshot. Later, he slunk away."

"You mean he's gone?"

"And without saying 'good-bye,'" deplored Mike. "It wasn't nice of him, was it?"

"This is getting absurd!"

"Yes. Curious and furtive behaviour of a cousin with a grievance," said Mike. "I suppose we dumped him in the room which used to be his, and he still had a key. I hope that he decided that it would be wiser not to face his uncle in the morning, and safer not to try to see you again! At least, I think we made him feel that there is nothing much the matter with your father yet."

"Is that why you stopped me speaking when he collapsed on the settee?" asked Julia. "Oh, of course, it is! But—Mike! What on earth made Fergus pretend to be drunk? And—great Scott, I'd forgotten. He came in very quietly, didn't he?"

"As quietly as he went out. Then he knocked into a chair, saw my shadow on the wall, and started his act. Any ideas?"

"I just can't understand it."

"Er—you haven't any particular soft spot for Fergus, have you?" asked Mike, cautiously.

"I think he's a detestable little—*oaf!*"

"Good! Apart from his grievance at being turned out—"

"He wasn't turned out."

"Oh, no. I'm sorry—he took himself off, and your father took him seriously. All the same, he has a grievance about this being your father's house instead of his. Has he any other grudge, do you know?"

"Isn't that big enough?" demanded Julia. "He has some justification for saying that morally it's his house, and I can never understand why Father didn't let him have it—it's not as if we're poor. The real truth is that Father has always hated moving, and he has two rooms upstairs crammed with his records. We've lived here for fifteen years, now. But it is a pretty ugly situation, isn't it?"

"It's complicated," Mike admitted. "Fergus hasn't gone about breathing threats, or anything like that, has he?"

"I think it's well known that he doesn't like Father."

"You mean, he's talked?"

"He might not have been drunk to-night, but he has been often enough, and it makes him talkative," said Julia. "As a matter of fact"—she hesitated, but resumed so quickly that Mike assumed that she felt in the mood for confidences—"he was all right until about three years ago. I don't mean that we fell on each other's neck, but he had sobered up a lot. Daddy and I thought that his father's death was the reason for that. Then he got engaged. She was a nice girl," Julia went on, "and I think Fergus worshipped her. She was killed in a car crash, and he's never really recovered from it. He started to drink again from then on, and it's a mystery to me how he's managed to hold down his job."

"Which is?"

"He's a draughtsman in a big electrical engineering works, and pretty good, I believe. What they call an 'ideas man,' too, although I think he's better at developing other people's ideas. I don't mean that cattily!" she added, quickly, "he's said as much himself. He usually keeps fairly sober when he's busy, but in slack periods he just drinks himself stupid. I knew he was away from the office—he's had a week's holiday. Well, that's about as much as you'll want to know about Fergus!" she added, standing up. "I'll tell Mrs. McFarlane to make up the spare-room for you. I won't be long."

"Thanks," said Mike.

He did not tell her that he intended to stay the night because he thought that there might be other visitors, but when she was asleep he left his room and sat in an easy-chair in a room opposite hers, so that he could watch the door. He dozed lightly, but there were no alarms. Before either she or Mrs. McFarlane was up, he went back to his own room and slept heavily for two hours.

The housekeeper woke him up, and gave him a cup of tea, wishing him a forbidding "good morning."

Mike had telephoned Craigie again before going to bed to mention the curious behaviour of Fergus Grey, and he had been satisfied by Craigie's assurance that Grey was being watched. He had been told to concentrate on the Hartleys, and, as he bathed and shaved he wondered what Julia's morning mood would be like.

He was puzzled by her behaviour of the previous night. At times she had behaved like an overwrought schoolgirl, but whenever she had come near the point of dressing him down for his deception, she had allowed herself to be sidetracked with ease. It might have been because she was affected by the sudden affliction of her father and was not her real self. If that were the only reason, he was likely to have a trying morning.

He went downstairs, and was met by Mrs. McFarlane, who was dressed in a flowered house-coat which made her large, brawny figure look formidable. Breakfast was served, and she said she was sure that he would not mind pouring out for himself. Her attitude suggested that she restrained herself with difficulty from telling him to go about his business, and her stony face did not relax when he said cheerfully:

"Of course not, Mrs. McFarlane! How is the invalid?"

"He had a *very* bad night," said Mrs. McFarlane, and took herself off.

She had cooked an excellent breakfast, the coffee was good, and there seemed no shortage of cream. Two morning papers were folded by his plate. Only his place was laid, and he was curious about Julia, and wondered whether she had been up before him or whether she was having breakfast in her room.

"She went out early," said Mrs. McFarlane, and her expression suggested that she was very pleased. Mike felt both disquieted and annoyed; true, his chief interest was in Hartley, but he should not have allowed Julia to go out without making some attempt to find out where she was going.

"When do you expect her back?" he asked.

"I don't know," said Mrs. McFarlane, and added: "When are you leaving, sir?"

"I'll discuss that with Miss Julia," said Mike, tartly.

She set her lips and turned away, leaving him in no doubt as to his unpopularity. Later, he went upstairs to the study, and found it locked. He tapped on Hartley's door, but received no answer. He had an uncomfortable feeling that he was being watched, and imagined several times that he heard the rustle of Mrs. McFarlane's starched house-coat. Ignoring the fancy, he went into the blinded man's room.

"Who is that?"

"Mike Errol," said Mike, quietly, "a friend of your daughter, Sir Basil."

"I understand that you have been taking a remarkable interest in my affairs," said Hartley, carefully. He did not open his eyes, and there was something eerie about the way he spoke while looking towards Mike. Moreover, his disapproval was as obvious as Mrs. McFarlane's, if less blunt. "When I feel better I shall require an explanation."

"I will gladly make it, sir," said Mike, "but I can assure you that I had only your interest in mind."

"That remains to be seen," said Hartley. "My daughter has related your story. She has gone to try to establish its accuracy."

"*What's* that?" gasped Mike.

"She has gone to visit an eminent friend of mine, who is acquainted with the Assistant Commissioner at Scotland Yard," said Hartley. "If you have lied, sir, I warn you that the consequences will be most unpleasant."

"Oh," said Mike, weakly.

He knew, now, why Julia's attitude had been non-committal and why she had gone off without giving him a chance to see her. He smiled wryly at the thought that he would have to confess to Craigie that he had been outwitted, but on the whole he was glad of the development. He felt at a loss to know what to say next. Hartley's helplessness affected him, and he wondered what was going on inside the economist's brilliant mind.

Hartley spoke again.

"My own doctor will be here in a short time, Mr. Errol, and I shall not want you present when he arrives."

"Of course not," said Mike. "I came up to find out whether there is anything I can do for you."

"There is nothing, thank you," said Hartley.

Mike was in the drawing-room when a small car drew up. From it stepped a short, lean man in a dark suit. Footsteps in the hall told Mike that someone else had seen the car turn into the short drive, and soon he heard Mrs. McFarlane's "Good morning, Doctor!" and from the drawing-room door watched Dr. Lewis.

It was then half-past ten.

Lewis was still with the patient when another car turned into the drive. This time Mike jumped to his feet, for he recognized the sleek lines of a Lagonda which belonged to Bruce Hammond, the leading active member of the Department. With Hammond on the spot, Mike's immediate troubles dissolved and he went to open the front door. This time Mrs. McFarlane did not appear, and he was prepared to welcome Bruce when he saw that Hammond was not alone. Julia was sitting beside him.

Mike's face dropped.

"Well, well!" he said, as he went forward, "life is still full of surprises. 'Lo, Bruce, how are you faring?"

Bruce Hammond was a sturdy man, clad in a well-cut brown suit, with a tanned face, brown hair, and a brown moustache clipped short and spreading over the whole of his upper lip. His brown eyes smiled good-humouredly.

"I think I've put you in good odour again," he said, as Julia joined them. "Haven't I, Miss Hartley? All right, Mike," he added, "Gordon would like to see you at the office as soon as you can make it—you don't mind?"

"If Julia would come with me," said Mike, "I'd love it!" He walked with them into the hall. "Is there anything else you want from me?"

"Not unless anything's happened since last night," said Hammond. He spoke with complete freedom, not at all disturbed by Julia's presence—and, although Julia was not smiling, she looked as if she were satisfied by her interview with an "eminent friend." "Miss Hartley went to the Yard, and they put her in touch with us, so she knows that we aren't trying to put anything across!"

Ten minutes later Mike was walking across the common towards the station. The sun was breaking through the mists, and he was perspiring gently. He felt quite happy at leaving the affairs of Lyddon House in the care of Bruce Hammond, and knew that Craigie would tell him the latest news when he reached the office in Whitehall. He was whistling to himself when he heard a train in the distance. As he was some way from the station, and Julia had told him that if he hurried he would just catch a fast train to Waterloo, he began to run, measuring his chances of being in time. Suddenly, he heard a shot, and, almost at the same moment, a bullet struck him in the shoulder. He stumbled and fell, numbed with surprise.

From behind a clump of bramble bushes, heavy with fruit, came a short, broad-shouldered man, who was putting a gun into his pocket.

4

THE MAN WHO ASKED QUESTIONS

No one else appeared to have taken any notice of the shot.

As the man approached, smiling faintly, the train rumbled into the station and came to a standstill. Cars passed on the road crossing the common, not two hundred yards away, and Mike thought he heard the whang of a golf ball.

He had eyes only for the thick-set man.

"I'm glad you've got the sense not to shout," that worthy said, reaching Mike and standing over him. His attitude was astonishing—nonchalant and self-possessed. "I shouldn't shout, Errol; if you do I'll put another bullet into you, and you won't know anything more about this world. No one will come to your rescue either, they're used to rabbit-shooting on the common. Where did I get you?"

"In the shoulder," said Mike.

"Are you carrying a gun?"

"Yes."

"*Henry!*" called the broad-shouldered man, raising his voice. "Henry—oh, there you are. Hurry up, man, we haven't got all day." The man called "Henry," an ordinary-looking individual with a rather frightened air, came hurrying from another clump of blackberry bushes. "Frisk him," said the first-comer, and stood aside, with his hand in his pocket and the gun jutting out against the cloth, while "Henry" went down on one knee and ran his hands through Mike's pockets. He found Mike's small automatic and a knife, and put them on the ground together with the rest of the contents of his pockets.

"That'll do," said the other.

"Okay, Mr. Brenn," said Henry, and slipped away, taking cover behind some bushes.

"Mr. Brenn" looked down into Mike's eyes. His own eyes were greenish-grey, large and wide-set, and he had a pleasant, reassuring face; he was the type of man whom Mike would normally have liked at first sight. His full lips were curved in a faint smile, and he seemed to find the whole situation amusing.

"I suppose you're congratulating yourself on having learned my name. You needn't—it's an assumed one. Brenn. Efficient, swift, handled well only by an expert—like the gun." He laughed. "Who are you working for, Errol?"

"I don't work for anyone," said Mike.

"Nonsense! And don't be awkward. You've done very well so far, and I'd much rather not cause you a lot of pain and hurt. Who are you working for? Mandino?"

"I don't know a man named Mandino," said Mike.

"Don't you?" Brenn frowned, his smile completely disappearing. "Now listen to me, Errol—you'd better not try to stall. If you don't talk, a body will be found on Woking Common, and it won't help you much even if the police find the murderer. They aren't likely to, but it won't concern you whether they do or not. Now, who are you working for?"

"No one," repeated Mike, firmly. "I have my own business."

"Your *own* business, eh?" said Brenn, curiously. "That's ambitious, Errol—and you don't stand a chance. Just what do you want from Hartley?"

"Can't you guess?" asked Mike.

He did not take the other's threat to murder him lightly, and his mind was working at speed, although the pain in his shoulder was beginning to obtrude upon the clearness of his thoughts. He knew that the other had jumped to a conclusion which was, obviously, inaccurate. His only course was to try to learn as much as he could by making evasive answers and by probing cautiously for information. "Mandino" was a name which he had never heard before. Already he knew that he was suspected of trying to "get something" from Hartley. Even those two items of information would be useful to Craigie if he could find a way of getting out of this. He wished the man would take his hand out of his pocket.

"Yes, I can guess," said Brenn, "only I'm not sure I believe you. I've never heard that you're in it before. The first time you cropped up was when you were seen to be hanging around Julia Hartley—I'm interested in people who attach themselves to her!" He laughed, unpleasantly. "Who was it who called last night?"

"A doctor, I think."

"You *think!*"

"Sir Basil was taken ill," Mike said. "They couldn't get hold of their family doctor, so they sent for another—I don't know his name. I'm not in the family confidence."

"Judging from the progress you've been making with Julia, I should have thought that you had them where you wanted them," said Brenn. "I could use a man like you, who knows his way about. You haven't got a chance, whether you're working on your own or for Mandino. What does he pay you?"

"I've never heard of Mandino, I tell you."

"I'm beginning to believe you," said Brenn. "All right, what profits do you make for yourself? Two thousand a year?"

"About," said Mike, now completely bewildered. The pain in his shoulder made his body go tense. He wanted to clench his teeth, but he fought against showing any sign of weakness.

"I'll pay you a level two thousand a year," said Brenn.

"For what?" demanded Mike, abruptly.

"Doing what you're told," said Brenn. "You're well in with Julia, and it will be worth two thousand a year to me for someone in that position. I haven't any time to waste," he went on brusquely. "Take it or leave it—I don't much mind. I'll have to satisfy myself that you aren't one of Mandino's smart young men, of course. Don't accept my offer if you are, because I wouldn't have any mercy on you." He laughed again, but there was an edge to his voice. "Come on, make up your mind."

"I'll have to know more about it," Mike said.

He moved, for the first time—and gasped with the pain in his shoulder.

"You can't have much more time," Brenn said, indifferently. "Make up your mind, Errol."

"What good am I to you with an arm like this?" snapped Mike, trying to sit up.

"That won't last long—haven't you heard of penicillin?" inquired Brenn, with the same indifferent air. "We can go into details later. The thing that matters just now is whether you will join me. If two thousand a year isn't enough, I could spring two and a half. That's my limit." He turned and raised his voice again. "Henry!"

"Yes, Mr. Brenn," said Henry, deferentially. He popped up from the bush as if he were a Jack-in-the-box, with his earnest face turned towards Mike.

"Bring the car as near as you can," said Brenn, turning back to Mike. "When the car arrives, you'll have to accept or refuse. I'm getting out of this. Please yourself—but don't run away with the idea that I shall let you go free; I can't afford to leave someone who might squeal." He took out the gun, a .32 automatic, glanced at it, and then smiled at Mike. "Don't think I'm going to take you on trust, either. I shall find out all about you before you get any work to do—but if you say yes, I'll see that you're well looked after in the interim. What is it to be?"

Mike drew a deep breath.

"All right, Brenn," he said, and smiled faintly. "I knew you were pretty tough, but I thought—" he stopped. "It doesn't matter. I'll need to get some things from my flat."

"Don't worry about that—I'll send for them," said Brenn. He seemed unaffected by Mike's decision and listened to the sound of a car engine getting nearer. "You can't get up on your own, I suppose?" He bent down, put an arm about Mike's shoulders, and helped him to his feet. Mike swayed and gasped, and his face went white. He bit his lips, and his head swam and the pain in his shoulder increased. Brenn took no notice but guided him towards the car, about twenty yards away. It was a large closed one. Brenn helped Mike into it, let him settle down in a corner, and then looked at his own hand, which was covered with blood.

"You certainly need attention for that shoulder," he said. "You'll get it, and you'll get a square deal from me, Errol, if you play fair. If you've got any tricks in mind, Heaven help you."

He did not smile; he did not put any great emphasis on the words, but Mike felt a cold shiver run through him, and forgot the pain; Brenn meant exactly what he said.

The car was driven slowly over the narrow road, bumping Mike so much that he had to clench his teeth. Brenn looked about him, and now had a self-satisfied smile on his face. It faded when a man stepped out of the gorse near the road and put up a hand, and he said sharply:

"Drive past, Henry! Errol, if you—"

He glanced at Mike, and then quickly away, for Henry applied the brakes so abruptly that both of them were thrown forward, and Mike exclaimed aloud. Yet Mike was glad of that interruption, glad that Brenn had been forced to look away—for he recognized the man who was standing in the middle of the road. It was impossible to drive round him, and Henry had not been able to obey orders.

Brenn snapped: "Keep your mouth shut, Errol." He leaned forward and wound down his window, glaring at the man, who had now left the middle of the road and was coming towards him. "What the devil do you mean by this, sir? My friend has injured himself in a fall. I am taking him to a doctor."

"Oh!" said the man by the window. He was fair-haired and would have been good-looking but for a broken nose. Whoever had broken his nose had done a good job of it. His name was Carruthers, he had worked for Gordon Craigie for many years, and he still managed to have a vacuous expression and to give the impression that he was a fool. "Oh!" he repeated, glancing curiously at Mike. "Well, *I* didn't know, did I? I wondered if you were going to Town, because I've just missed a train."

"I have no time to waste," snapped Brenn.

"Oh, nor have I," said Carruthers, promptly. "I'm in a heck of a hurry as a matter of fact—a date." He beamed. "I would appreciate it, old chap—will a little inducement help? I mean, I don't want something for nothing? Or oughtn't your friend to go to the local hospital?"

"His own doctor will attend to him," said Brenn, and to Mike's surprise, added: "I can take you as far as Marble Arch. Will that suit you?"

"Oh, splendid!" cried Carruthers, "splendid!" He began to open the door, but Brenn stopped him and said:

"Sit next to the driver, please."

"Oh, gladly, gladly!" burbled Carruthers. "Extremely good of you to help, sir—especially in the circs." He climbed in next to Henry, and babbled on: "I say, your friend *does* look peaky. Poor chap! Perhaps he'd like a cigarette?" He took a cigarette from a slim gold case and handed it to Mike, who sat back with his eyes narrowed and with mixed feelings. Carruthers might give the truth away, but on the other hand he might make the difference between his complete and only partial success.

Brenn refused a cigarette. Carruthers lit Mike's and his own, and babbled on and on.

Robert Carruthers often admitted that one of the surprising things Gordon Craigie had taught him was that he had a resourceful mind. Craigie, who did not employ fools, knew that Carruthers liked to pretend to be one, even in the Department; of all the facetious young men who worked for him, Carruthers was certainly the most unpredictable. When Carruthers telephoned to say that he must see Craigie immediately, Craigie knew that it was not a matter of minor importance, and told him to come at once.

"Where are you?" he asked.

"In the Edgware Road, old chap," said Carruthers, "outside Number 101g. If you've someone wandering around waiting for something to do, I'd send him along, if I were you. Can do?"

"Yes," said Craigie.

"Splendid!" said Carruthers. "Tell him to be in the lounge of the Cumberland in half an hour's time."

He rang off, and in the office Craigie replaced the receiver and looked across at Loftus, who was sitting at a large desk.

"Tell Mark Errol to go to 101g Edgware Road, will you," he said, "and tell him to give us a ring for more precise information later. Carruthers wasn't explicit. I fancy he thought he might be overheard. And Merrick had better see Carruthers in the Cumberland lounge—at once."

Precisely an hour later, a green light glowed in the mantelpiece of the Department office. It indicated that someone outside was pressing the bell, and since only two or three men, apart from Department members, knew where to find the bell, Craigie assumed that it was Carruthers. It was. The fair-haired man entered the office and cast a beaming smile about him before helping himself to a cigarette from a box on the mantelpiece and lowering his long form into an easy-chair in front of the fire.

The large office, which was nearly twice as long as it was wide, had one-half quite different from the other. The end away from the fireplace was barely furnished; there were dictaphones, steel files, two large steel desks, some steel paper-baskets, and a dozen telephones in neat array on one side of each desk. Each telephone was a different colour, and lately Craigie had arranged for a small light to show when a bell rang, so that he could pick on the right telephone without delay.

The other end might have been the lounge of any bachelor's flat. A large cupboard, with many shelves and drawers, was always crammed with oddments, varying from food to items of apparel. Only Craigie and, more lately, Loftus, knew just where to find whatever was wanted. By the side of the cupboard was a bed, let in the wall—and recently another had been installed next to it for Loftus. Each man had a flat of his own in the West End, but those flats were unused for days on end.

Carruthers told Craigie and Loftus what he had seen and heard. He had missed little, for the clumps of bushes which had hidden Henry and Brenn so effectively had also hidden him. He told of his decision to hold the car up and beg a lift, because, he said, it was the only way in which he could find out what had really happened to Mike, who was wounded in the shoulder. Mike had given him no sign of recognition, not even a wink, and so Carruthers had assumed that he did not want to be helped just then—obviously, because he hoped to get away with "working" for Mr. Brenn.

"Mike handled that well," said Craigie thoughtfully. "We might have something to work on already, too—Brenn and Mandino, and they want something which Hartley might be able to give them." He glanced at Loftus, who was filling his pipe and eyeing Carruthers. "Any ideas, Bill?"

"I'm sitting back in astonishment," said Loftus, sober-faced. "I didn't think Mike or Carry had it in them—they're improving! No, I can't say that I've any ideas, beyond doing the usual things. Bruce will get whatever there is to get from the Hartleys, I think, although the quicker he knows of the latest development, the better. I don't envy him handling Julia," he added with a grin, "her little trick of coming straight to the Yard must have knocked the stuffing out of Mike. How badly is he hurt, Carry?"

"He looked pretty washed-out," said Carruthers. "I don't think he'll be in action again for a week or two, but he might slip a message out to us. By the way, didn't I hear some mention of a red-haired customer named Grey—Hartley's nephew."

"Yes—why?" said Craigie.

"Curious thing," said Carruthers, thoughtfully. "The great mind has been working slowly. Fergus and Grey is an unusual combination. I used to play cricket with a Fergus Grey, with the Surrey Wanderers. Quite a stylist, my Fergus, with a tendency to lift the ball too much, and he had a really nice googly. I remember, once—"

"Was he red-haired?" asked Loftus.

"As red as they come," said Carruthers, and added modestly: "I had a brainwave, and dubbed him Carrots. The name stuck, too. That's what originality does for you! Amiable individual, with an enormous capacity for beer, but whisky knocked him over in a wink. There couldn't be two Carrots Greys, could there?"

"It isn't likely," said Craigie. "I think you'd better try to get in touch with him, Carry—Mark doesn't know him, and it'll be better than striking up an acquaintance. You'll have to be careful, because Brenn and his chauffeur would recognize you. If they catch sight of you hovering near Grey while Mike's with them—"

Carruthers waved a hand airily.

"For once, the great G. C. can't see the wood for the trees," he said. "After all, I *live* near Lyddon House. I mean, I can pretend that I do, and so there would be nothing surprising in my turning up and asking for a lift. There's a little guest house not very far from the common—do you know Martha Dale?"

"Why should I know Martha Dale?" asked Craigie.

"She's the type of person people do know," said Carruthers, grandly. "She has thousands of acquaintances, I'd say, and she's a pet. There was a time when, with about fifty others, I hoped she'd marry me, but she went off with some long-shanked, sober-faced individual who owned this house. He lost all his money—he was in rubber—and part of a foot in the bargain. So Martha rallied round, they turned the house into a guest house, and—what I mean to say," said Carruthers, "is that Martha won't mind swearing that I've lived there, on and off, for quite a long time. So we should be all right." He regarded Loftus, and frowned slightly. "Why the deep scowl, Bill?"

"It's all too easy," said Loftus, "and I don't trust coincidences."

"There's no coincidence about me knowing Martha Dale," said Carruthers, with a greater show of spirit. "It just happens that Hartley lives near there and that I'm a Surrey man myself. Don't let him stop you from using my talents," he implored, looking at Craigie. "It's a gift from the gods. I don't mind admitting that I had to do some brain-storming to work it all out, but the Fergus started it. Well, Gordon?"

"Get in touch with Fergus Grey," said Craigie, quietly.

Soon afterwards, Craigie put other agents and the police on to searching for the man Mandino, but, despite the uncommon name, it was not as easy as he hoped. There were over thirty Mandinos in London, some English, some Italian and some Americans. It was a curious fact that, hard though the police and the agents worked, it was a long time before it was discovered that one of the men so named, who lived in Chiswick, was blind. Had Craigie learned that earlier, he might have been able to start a new line of investigation very quickly.

As it was, he remained in ignorance for too long.

5

TWO WEEKS OF SPADE WORK

Craigie was not sorry that very little happened during the next two weeks. It gave him time to place his men where he thought they would be most useful, and it also gave time for the various situations to develop. Yet he, Loftus and the others were conscious of a tension; it was as if they were waiting for something to blow up; when it did, it would cause a sensation.

Nothing was heard from Mike Errol.

The man who called himself Brenn did not stay at the house in Edgeware Road all the time, but seemed to use it as a *pied-à-terre* whenever he was in London. Callers often went there, including a tall, spindly individual who affected a Victorian garb and always carried a Gladstone bag. The betting among those of Craigie's agents who watched the house was that he was a doctor. On his third appearance he was followed to South Kensington, where he had a flat. He was known there as Mr. Gabriel Witherspoon, and no one seemed to know whether he had medical qualifications; he was not in the Medical

Register under that name. Except when he visited the Edgware Road house he rarely left his flat, but he was kept under constant watch.

Sir Basil Hartley remained at Lyddon House, and was being treated by Faversham. There was no improvement in his sight, nor in that of the other three victims. A knowledgeable individual from the Home Office had visited him soon after his affliction, and told him a little about Bruce Hammond and Mike Errol. Hartley had agreed to co-operate, but could offer no information. Bruce Hammond, as a friend of Julia's, was often at the house, which was closely watched from the outside. To her surprise, Mrs. McFarlane found that her advertisement for a servant, which had remained unanswered for so long, brought a middle-aged, sorrowful-looking man to the house. He applied for the post, declaring that he was not allowed to do heavy work because he had a weak heart.

Mrs. McFarlane made it clear that in other times she would not have considered employing him, and supposed that he was strong enough to carry buckets of coal. He said that he was. He was engaged, subject to references, which proved to be excellent. He gave his name as Forbeson. Moreover, his name was Forbeson, and he had worked for Department "Z" for a long time.

To Mrs. McFarlane's further surprise, he proved a first-class servant; in spite of the invalid, the arrangements at Lyddon House ran very smoothly.

Julia spent a lot of time helping her father. Bruce Hammond, that brown-eyed, brown-haired man who inspired instant liking in nearly everyone whom he met—he was a quiet, self-effacing individual, very unlike many other leading agents of the Department—thought that Julia was more worried than she admitted. Whether her anxiety was caused by the sudden blindness of her father, or whether there was something deeper behind it, he could not be sure, but he felt that she applied herself to the task of becoming her father's eyes, and did not find it easy.

After the first few days, Hartley began to pick up the threads of work again.

The other six members of his Committee were not affected, although each was watched wherever he went. The Committee was sitting on an inquiry into the practicability of a number of recommended measures of automation and economic expansion, but the exact details of the scope of the inquiry were known only to a few. Craigie was one of those few, and he confided in Hammond and Loftus just fourteen days after Mike Errol's disappearance.

"It's pretty ambitious," he said, sitting back in an easy-chair and filling his pipe, which drooped from his mouth to his chest. "Rebuilding, road construction, electronics—but nothing to justify what is happening."

"What is Hartley's speciality?" Loftus asked.

"He is the economist of the party, working on the costs. Although sponsored by the Government, it's a non-party, non-political inquiry. Why its members should be victimised is beyond me." After a pause, Craigie went on anxiously: "It's curious that nothing at all has happened since Mike disappeared. The obvious thing was to leave him alone and let him work out the situation, but if he let anything slip in delirium they might have killed him. That would explain why they're keeping so quiet."

"I don't think you'll have to worry about that," said Hammond, standing up. "They believe they're on to something good in Mike! Well, I'll slip down to Woking to see Julia. By the way, what about the report on the Dales?"

"They're all right," said Craigie.

He had received two reports. Dale had been in the R.A.F. and had had a bad crash. As a result, he had been in hospital for months, and his face, badly burned, had been treated with plastic surgery, so that he had a rather set expression, but otherwise looked normal. He had lost part of one foot, and limped because of it. The house, which was now the Guest House, had belonged to an uncle of his and he had inherited it some years before, according to his own statement. Craigie had closely checked his R.A.F. record, and Martha's past.

The Dales, it seemed, were likely to be useful.

In the opinion of Robert Carruthers, things were dull; Fergus Grey was also dull.

Carruthers was acutely conscious of the inaction which followed his living at the Guest House because of Martha Dale. He had told the others that he had once been her suitor, but they had not taken him seriously. The truth was, he now admitted, that he had not taken himself seriously enough. Now that he saw a great deal of her, he was reminded vividly of the time when he had hoped that she would marry him. It was not easy to live there and to be in regular touch with her, only too aware of her affection for Jim Dale, whose set face rarely reflected emotion but whom Carruthers could not help but like.

As for Fergus Grey, he was a man with a grievance which he aired whenever he was in his cups, which was most evenings. He helped to take Carruthers' mind off Martha, when he was propped up against the bar of the Gorse and Briar, a friendly little hostelry not far from the Guest House. The Guest House itself had no name, but Martha and her husband insisted on the capital letters.

Grey lived at the Gorse and Briar.

When Carruthers first met him, as if casually, he said that he was having a rest cure, but omitted to say from what. From then on he spent a lot of time with Grey, who seemed to need a confidant.

Everything that Grey said about his relationship with the Hartleys amplified what Julia had already told Mike Errol. His grudge was against Sir Basil more than Julia, although he gave it as his opinion that Julia was a stuck-up little baggage who had no thought for anyone but herself.

He returned to the subject of Julia on the fourteenth evening, when Carruthers had succeeded in enticing him away from the Gorse and Briar, and they were sitting in the comfortable lounge of the Guest House. None of the other residents was in, for there was a particularly good show on at a Woking cinema. When there was a ring at the front-door bell, Martha Dale walked quickly from the private lounge and opened the door.

Carruthers was listening to Grey with half an ear, and heard a man's voice, which was vaguely familiar. He tried to shut out what Grey was saying, and heard the man say:

"I am so sorry to worry you, but is Mr. Fergus Grey here, please?"

"Yes," said Martha Dale, clearly, "he's with Mr. Carruthers. Do come in." The door closed, the man murmured his appreciation, and Martha, whose mop of wavy, black hair was cut in a bob, put her round, innocent-looking face round the door.

"Mr. Grey, there's someone to see you. Shall I show him in? Oh, *hang* it!" Martha exclaimed, "I forgot to ask his name." Her head disappeared. "It's Mr.—"

"Crow," said the man whose voice was familiar.

"Crow," repeated Grey, standing up quickly. He tried to hide his alarm, but failed lamentably. "What the blazes does *he* want?"

Carruthers looked blank.

"He's a Mr. Crow," said Martha, popping her head round the door again. "Shall I—"

"No, I'll see him in the hall," said Grey, quickly.

He went out, and closed the door; Martha's footsteps faded. Carruthers stood up and approached the door quietly, but he could hear only a mutter of voices. He opened the door an inch, very softly, and he was in time to hear Grey say in a low-pitched voice:

"I've said no, and I mean no. That's final."

"I hope you won't stick to it," said Crow.

Although his voice was also low-pitched, it gave Carruthers a shock, for it belonged to the man who also called himself Brenn. The pleasant voice was exactly the same, and Carruthers could see the shadow of his stocky figure on the wall.

"I shall stick to it!" snapped Grey, in a louder voice, "and I resent you coming here. You might at least have had the decency to wait until I was back at the pub. Do you mind going?"

Brenn's voice seemed to have a lilt in it.

"You know, Grey you're a very foolish young man. You can make a lot of money, and—"

"Good night," said Grey clearly, and Carruthers heard the door open. He did not go into the hall at once, but waited for Brenn's reaction.

"I hope you will not make it necessary for me to warn you," began Brenn, "that, unless you are more amenable, I shall be compelled to—"

His voice was very low-pitched, but Carruthers could hear every word. He was waiting on the next when there was a sudden thump, a gasp and a thud, as if someone had hit the floor. Still cautious, he put his head round the door. Brenn was on his knees, and getting up slowly, glaring into Grey's eyes with an expression of unbridled malignance.

"I say, old man," said Carruthers, calling from the room, "are you all right?"

Both men ignored him, and Brenn said:

"Very well, Grey, you'll hear about this."

"If you don't get out, I'll throw you out!" snapped Grey. "And don't come back. If I see you again, Mr. Ruddy Crow, I'll break your neck!"

Brenn went out and Grey slammed the door.

From a room on the other side of the square hall popped Martha's mop of hair, and her tall husband peered down curiously from the landing.

"I say, old chap—" began Carruthers.

Fergus Grey looked towards but not at him. He did not seem to see him or either of the others. In his eyes there was an expression so akin to terror that it made Carruthers step forward swiftly, and brought a gasp from Martha's lips. Then, without a word, Grey turned and went out of the house, and they heard him stumbling along the path.

The man on the landing came hurrying downstairs. Carruthers had seen before that he had a remarkable ability to move swiftly in spite of his injured foot. In the fortnight he had lived at the Guest House, Carruthers had come to admire Jim Dale, and he was not surprised when that worthy said:

"A spot of escort duty, Carry?"

"Yes, let's," said Carruthers.

Carruthers had a pocket torch which cast a long and powerful beam along the path, and he caught sight of Grey, moving swiftly towards the common. Side by side, Carruthers and Dale hurried in his wake, but although they walked for half an hour, by which time Dale began to limp badly and admitted *sotto voce* that he would soon have to have a rest, nothing happened. Grey walked on as if he did not know or care where he was going, but eventually he turned back and went to the Gorse and Briar.

Dale and Carruthers stopped outside.

"Odd show," said Dale, breathing hard.

"Very odd," said Carruthers, thoughtfully. "Did you hear all that was said?"

"No, but I gathered the man called Crow was being uppish."

"Did you see Grey's face?"

"Yes. Not pleasant," said Dale, slowly. "I've seen that look on the faces of other people who have been terrified—right word?" he asked laconically.

"I can't think of a better."

"Er—how well do you know Grey? Well enough to ask him what it was all about?"

"We-ell, I don't know," said Carruthers, indecisively. He had asked the Dales to say that he had been there for some weeks, and obtained their promise, but had offered no explanation. "It would be a bit of a nerve, don't you think? I mean, it is no business of ours now that we know nothing has happened."

"You mean you don't want me to ask questions," said Dale, with a ghost of a laugh. Carruthers could not see his face, and he was surprised at the words. "Please yourself, but if I can lend a hand, say so. Oh—and don't think you'll get away with being the fool you look!"

Carruthers said: "Oh!" and sounded blank.

"Because I happen to—" began Dale, only to be stopped, for Carruthers gripped his arm swiftly and painfully, conveying an unmistakable warning.

Carruthers went on talking, and all the time he was on the alert. When he had stopped Dale he had heard a sound near by, one which might have been a footstep. Now he was trying to distinguish objects in the darkness. He could make out the doorway of the pub, the windows and the shrubs which grew on either side of the door. Farther away he could see the inn sign. The wall of the Gorse and Briar was cream-washed, and anything dark showed up against it.

He saw the figure of a man near one of the windows.

He moved towards it swiftly, confident that he himself could not be seen, for there was no light background behind him. Suddenly he pounced.

"Keep still, little man," he whispered, "or—"

The threat was not uttered, for the little man caved in without making a further attempt to get away. Dale came up and spoke in a wondering voice.

"What have you found?"

"One small human being, lurking in suspicious circumstances," said Carruthers, lightly. "I'd rather like a word with him someplace less public than this."

"We're only ten minutes away from home," said Dale, "so bring him along."

"Well, I don't know—"

"Bring him along," insisted Dale. "and if you're going to babble about the risk involved, forget it."

"The thing is, I'm worried about Grey," said Carruthers, thoughtfully. "This little customer might have been after him, but there remains Crow."

From the darkness there came a voice, low-pitched but familiar.

"All right, Carry—you go ahead." It was Bruce Hammond.

Dale stiffened; and then the little man, who had remained so limp in Carruthers' grip, made a bolt for freedom. He timed it well, for Hammond's voice had taken Carruthers off his guard. As the man freed himself, however, Carruthers shot out a foot, and tripped him up. There was a heavy thud against the cobbled courtyard, and the man winced. Carruthers switched on his torch, to make sure that he got a grip on his arm, and hauled him to his feet before putting the torch out.

Dale said nothing.

Carruthers, satisfied that Hammond knew what he was doing, led the way to the Guest House. He pushed the little man ahead of him, while holding his arm in a half-Nelson; he had no further trouble.

Martha opened the door before they reached the porch. She eyed the newcomer with a blank face, and Carruthers was surprised as well as puzzled by her apparent lack of curiosity. She said nothing as he hustled the little man up to his own room, with Dale limping after him. Inside, they closed the door and let the man relax on the bed.

"Well, Henry," said Carruthers.

It was Brenn's chauffeur, as he had suspected. The man looked frightened, pale, and dishevelled, and there was a bruise on his cheek and a cut on his hand, where he had fallen. He stared at Carruthers without speaking, his sensitive lips working.

"What were you going to do with Grey?" asked Carruthers lightly.

"N-n-nothing!"

"What a lot of trouble you were taking to do nothing," said Carruthers, with his head on one side. "Now, Henry, you must be sensible. If you tell the truth we'll let you go, and you'll have nothing to worry about provided it's the whole truth. What were you going to do with Grey?"

"N-*nothing!*"

"An obstinate young man," said Carruthers, with a sigh. Without warning he moved his right hand forward and snapped his fingers under Henry's nose, making the man back away. He leaned too far, lost his balance, and cracked his head on the wall.

"You *are* having a rough time," said Carruthers, shaking his head sadly, "and it will get worse unless you tell the truth, you know. Why did you follow Grey?"

Henry stared at him with frightened eyes, but set his lips stubbornly. Carruthers doubted whether the man could be persuaded to talk while he was at the house, and he looked his annoyance. At the same time he took a penknife from his pocket and opened one blade with great deliberation. Henry's eyes widened, and he tried to cringe away. Dale kept his face straight, and Carruthers whetted the blade on the palm of his hand.

"I don't *like* doing this," he said, "and—"

"You won't do it," said a voice from the door.

Carruthers half-turned, putting his right hand to his pocket for his gun as he caught sight of Brenn standing by the door. As he moved, Henry came from the bed like a bullet, and crashed into him, carrying him to the floor. Dale backed away from the automatic in Brenn's hand.

6

THE CALMNESS OF MR. BRENN

The astonishing thing about Brenn was his composure. He looked unruffled, and there was even a smile on his lips, as if he were suggesting that the gun was the greatest joke in the world.

Carruthers did not try to get to his feet.

"Why, hallo!" he said.

"Hallo," said Brenn, as if humouring a child. "Oh, Dale—I locked your wife in the closet beneath the stairs; she will come to no harm if you behave yourself, but she won't be able to summon help. I happen to know that all your other guests have gone to the pictures, and they won't be home for an hour. Don't run away with the idea that help might come unexpectedly. Even if it did, I have a man downstairs. He will take care of anyone who should arrive."

Dale stared at him, but said nothing.

"You do make good arrangements, don't you?" said Carruthers, wondering why Dale took it so calmly.

Brenn smiled at him.

"How good they are you don't yet know," he said. "Listen, Carruthers: when did you first see me?"

Carruthers grinned. "About a fortnight ago, wasn't it? When you were good enough to give me a lift!" His grin broadened. "You didn't know you were nurturing a viper in your bosom, did you, Mr. Brenn?"

Brenn said: "How long have you known Errol?"

"Errol?" echoed Carruthers, frowning. "I don't know anyone named—oh, I remember! That friend of yours whom you were taking to see a doctor. As a matter of fact, I only knew that he was keeping company with Julia Hartley. What's happened to him?"

Brenn snapped: "I've had enough fooling! Are you one of Craigie's men?"

Carruthers stared, his expression hardening. Brenn looked satisfied with the effect of his words, and Carruthers hoped that he had taken the right course. He had decided to try to convince Brenn that Mike Errol was not a friend or associate of his; if he also denied all knowledge of Craigie, he would probably defeat his own ends.

"So you are," murmured Brenn. "Well, well—I had heard that he was taking an interest, which is very foolish of him, but I didn't realise that he had started as long as a fortnight ago. How long has Errol worked for him?"

Carruthers drew in his breath.

"I've told you all I know about Errol," he said, standing up slowly, "and if you expect me to say any more, you're unlucky. I'm not talking."

"I don't even know that I want you to talk," said Brenn, "now that you've confirmed that Craigie is in this, I'm quite happy." He smiled as if he meant exactly what he said. "You can tell Craigie that nothing he or his men do will make any difference—is that clear?"

Carruthers shrugged his shoulders.

"I think the lesson has been well rammed home," said Brenn, "and I mean it. Henry, look through all the drawers."

Until then Henry's gaze had been fixed on Carruthers. Now he started and moved to the dressing-table. With bewildering speed he took out the contents of each drawer, examined each article, and replaced it neatly. In spite of his speed, the task took nearly a quarter of an hour. All the time the others were standing quite still. Dale did not once speak, a fact which made Carruthers curious, for Dale was the type of man who would make some effort to hit back. Certainly it was not like him to be easily intimidated.

Henry finished at last, and said:

"Nothing, Mr. Brenn."

"I suppose even Craigie's men have some elementary common sense," said Brenn. "All right, we'll go. Just to make sure you don't make a nuisance of yourself, Carruthers, I'm going to put a hole through your thigh, and—"

A sudden banging on a door downstairs interrupted him. He did not take his gaze from Carruthers or Dale, although his gun moved up a little. Henry slipped past him and went on to the landing, while the banging on the door grew louder. Carruthers saw the faint smile on Dale's lips and knew that he had expected some such development, but neither of them had expected Henry's sudden shout:

"Mr. Brenn—the police, they're—"

He darted back into the room and slammed the door. Carruthers jumped forward at Brenn, taking a chance. Brenn kicked him viciously, and sent him over, while Henry kicked out at Dale and brought him thudding down. Then the two assailants darted towards the window, and while Brenn pulled aside the curtains Henry thrust the window up. Men's voices sounded outside the door, which shook as someone flung himself against it.

Henry climbed out and appeared to drop down without a second thought. Neither Carruthers nor Dale had recovered themselves before Brenn was also out of the window, but as he turned and faced them, crouching, he pointed his gun towards Carruthers, who was on his knees. Carruthers flung himself forward, and a bullet went over his head and struck the wall by the door. A moment later the door burst open, and Brenn dropped from sight.

A man in plain clothes and two uniformed policemen entered the room and rushed to the window, but they could only see where the light shone immediately in front of them.

One of the policemen began to climb out, but he lacked the confidence of the other two who had gone this way, and it was some time before he disappeared from sight. The man in plain clothes was looking at Dale.

"What's the trouble, Mr. Dale?"

"Who—" began Carruthers.

"It's all right, Carry," said Dale. "Brenn made a mistake when he locked Martha in the cupboard—that's where the public telephone is! You'd better talk to Sergeant Whitehead, hadn't you? Oh, Whitehead—Mr. Robert Carruthers. The sergeant is from the Woking police, Bob, and we're old friends."

Carruthers smoothed his flaxen hair.

"When in contact with the police," he said, like a man repeating a lesson, "request the said police to communicate with Superintendent Miller, of Scotland Yard—they're my instructions. Would you mind, Sergeant?"

Whitehead, a large, athletic-looking man, looked disappointed, but said that he would telephone Miller immediately. He left a uniformed policeman in the room, and went downstairs, but Dale followed him. The key was on the outside of the door of the cupboard under the stairs, and when he opened it, Martha came out breathlessly.

"Did it work?" she gasped. "Oh, Mr. Whitehead!—so it did!" She beamed, and then brushed a smudge of white from her arm, and looked appealingly into her husband's face. "Darling, we *must* do something about that cupboard, the whitewash comes off every time anyone leans against it. I'm sure we'll have a complaint if we don't alter it. *Do* be careful, Mr. Whitehead!"

Whitehead was already dropping coins into the box.

Ten minutes later he came from the telephone, disappointed but quite satisfied with his talk with the Yard.

"Well," he said, "I suppose there's no point in me staying."

"Please yourself, old chap," said Carruthers. "At least, you've the satisfaction of having scared off the bad men—it was a smart idea to have left a man banging on the front door as if you were trying to get in, while you were actually halfway up the stairs. Wasn't there one of Mr. Brenn's young gentlemen downstairs, too? Martha said two people came in, and Brenn said—"

"There was a man in the porch," said Whitehead, looking troubled. "I took him by surprise and clouted him. I thought he was right out, but he came round and slunk away. The man I left downstairs was a bit slow, I'm afraid. By the way, shall I leave a couple of men outside in case you're visited again?"

"That's a thought," said Carruthers. "Many thanks."

Whitehead gave his men instructions, and went off. Carruthers and Dale stood in the lounge eyeing each other, as if each was determined to make the other speak first.

"Carry owes us an explanation or two, I think," Dale said at last.

Carruthers smiled diffidently. Martha's eyes, filled with concern, affected him far more than they appeared to affect Dale. He thought that if he did not conquer his feelings for Martha he would have to ask Craigie to shift him. As it was, he disliked what he had to say very much indeed.

"Not really," he said. "I was just doing a job of work, keeping an eye on Fergus Grey. Er—sorry about this, old chap, but I'll have to report, you know, and my High-ups will want to know why you behaved with such remarkable aplomb, and how you guessed that I wasn't on a rest cure. I mean, you *did* know, didn't you?"

"Mind you," said Carruthers, sitting in Gordon Craigie's office early the next morning, "I don't think that Dale had any real information, and I think he told the truth. Just after I joined the Department—that's seven years ago—I was taking Martha here and there, and, apparently in a moment of indiscretion, I hinted to her that I was on a special job. And Dale says that she had never mentioned it to him until I came to take the room at the Guest

House. Then she remembered it and told him, and they read between the lines and assumed that I was on business. Er—for my seven-year-old sin, I'm sorry."

For once he was not smiling.

Craigie nodded. "It's reasonable enough, but Dale seems to have acted with considerable presence of mind."

"He's a resourceful customer," admitted Carruthers, "and as for Martha—" he smiled. "She has to be known to be believed! You'd think she was woolly-minded, and that she couldn't add two and two together, but she's nobody's fool. They *might* be useful if the scene still centres about Woking."

"Well, I've had them checked up," said Craigie. He went on: "Hammond was at the Gorse and Briar, because someone had telephoned that Brenn himself had left the Edgware Road house and was on his way to Woking. He arrived at the pub with Henry. He went inside. Henry stayed outside, and you caught him. Brenn left, obviously to come to your Guest House, and Hammond lost him in the black-out, but decided that it would be wise not to go too far away."

"Which is where Bruce slipped up," said Carruthers. "If he'd followed Brenn—"

Craigie shook his head.

"He stayed at hand to look after Grey, and rightly. The fact that no one else saw Grey and that the night was quite uneventful as far as he was concerned, doesn't matter. We're not likely to get anything out of Brenn, even if we catch him. I don't imagine that he is a talker. But it's obvious that Grey is important to him, that Grey has worked for him. So we must keep Grey safe until the right moment comes to question him."

"I suppose so," conceded Carruthers. "I'll take it back. Well, what's next?"

Craigie shrugged. "It's not at all a satisfactory business. Brenn and his man completely disappeared. They did not return to Edgware Road last night, and no one has been there this morning."

"Isn't it time we had a look at that place?" asked Carruthers. "If I'm right—that is, if I pulled off what I tried to last night, I've cleared Mike of suspicion of being one of us. Was I right to try?" He looked hopeful.

"Quite right," said Craigie.

"Even at the cost of confirming Brenn's suspicion that you're on the job?"

"Yes," said Craigie. "The most important thing at the moment is to make sure that Mike has every possible chance of worming himself into Brenn's good graces. A lot depends on Mike."

Since Craigie seemed satisfied, Carruthers was happier, and felt that he could ask:

"Just what is behind it, Gordon?"

Craigie shrugged. "I don't know, and none of us have more than an inkling. It seems to revolve largely about Hartley and the Commission. What we've got to try to avoid is acting too quickly. We might only catch the people on the surface, and not find out who is really behind it."

"So you think it's big?"

Craigie smiled. "Yes, but I've been known to be wrong!"

"Not often," said Carruthers. "Well, what shall I do next?"

"Go back and find out what Fergus Grey's mood is like," said Craigie. "If there's any need to change your angle, I'll let you know. Oh—Mark Errol will be working down there for a bit, so you'll probably come across him."

"Right," said Carruthers.

He went back to Woking by car, and was very thoughtful all the way. He knew that Mike and Mark Errol were almost inseparable, and he could imagine that Mark was finding the continued absence of his cousin a great strain. The worst of it was that Mike might not be alive. He was inclined to think that Craigie was wrong in not trying to find out what was happening in the Edgware Road house, but he had often thought that Craigie was wrong, only to find him justified by events.

Meanwhile, he wondered whether Fergus Grey would be himself again.

The man who was known as Witherspoon opened his black bag, just an hour after Carruthers had gone back to Woking, and looked at his patient. Mike Errol had seen him twice a day for the first week of his incarceration, and once a day thereafter, but had not once seen the man smile. Witherspoon's face seemed like parchment: it was yellow and leathery, and with lines which looked as if they were carved from stone. His craggy features and jutting eyebrows gave him a forbidding appearance, and his close-set eyes were always hard. He was bald on the top of his head, but had a good crop of bushy hair at the sides.

"Good morning," said Witherspoon. He asked no questions, but began to unfasten the bandages; Mike was stripped to the waist in readiness. The wound was almost healed, and Witherspoon pressed it gently, looking into the patient's face. Mike said nothing, and Witherspoon did not ask whether it hurt; he seemed to assume that it did not.

"I shall put on no more dressings," he said, "but it must be kept covered and you must not use your arm very much for a week or more."

"Otherwise, it's all right," said Mike, with relief. "All I want now is plenty of fresh air—when can I go out?"

"That is not in my hands," said Witherspoon. "I shall not need to see you again. I will leave a prescription for medicine downstairs, and you will find that will help you. Good morning."

"Good morning," echoed Mike.

Witherspoon went out and closed and locked the door.

Mike looked at it ruefully as he stepped across the room and began to put on a shirt. It was not easy, for his arm was stiff, but he managed it without too much trouble. He examined himself critically in the mirror. He had never been fat, but the past fortnight had made him painfully thin, and although he had walked about the room he still felt weak and knew that he would not be able to trust himself to walk far. His skin was pasty, and there were dark rings under his eyes. The only real cure was fresh air; he longed for an hour or two outside, lounging in a chair with the sun shining on him. He felt lifeless, disinterested, and easily depressed. He wondered whether it were intentional, whether they were trying to reduce his powers of resistance so as to exert pressure when there was little chance that he would be able to deceive them.

That possibility preyed on his mind.

He lit a cigarette—he was kept well supplied with them—and leaned against an easy chair. Except for stiffness, he was hardly aware of his injury. He found himself brooding again over Brenn, over Julia Hartley, and all that had preceded his capture, but, as always, his mind roamed. Somewhere in the north of England Regina Brent was waiting for a letter from him. Regina was his fiancée, and she knew what work he did. She would understand that work had made it impossible for him to write, but that would not stop her from worrying.

She might think him dead; and so might the others.

He turned round abruptly, for the door opened—and he stepped back in astonishment as a man dressed in black entered, carrying a top-hat. The apparition was so startling that Mike gaped.

He could just see the stairs; up them two men were carrying something which looked like a long, narrow box. It was not a box, but a coffin. Mike stiffened, and snapped:

"What's this?"

"Now, take it easy, sir, take it easy!" said the man with the top-hat. He was red-faced, plump and smiling, and his voice was unctuous. "Not many people who go into a box like that come out again, now, do they? No, they don't! It's quite all right, you'll be able to breathe."

"What the devil are you talking about?" demanded Mike.

"Why, the box," said the red-faced man. He held out his hand. "Have you ever seen one of these, I wonder?" Mike stared down— and with a swift movement the red-faced man jabbed a hypodermic needle into his forearm. Mike snatched his hand away and backed to the window, every vestige of colour drained from his cheeks.

"Now, don't you worry," said the undertaker, soothingly. "You'll be as right as ninepence when you come out, don't you worry!" He stood back, smiling widely, while the other men brought the coffin into the room and rested it on the bed. They did not seem to realise the macabre nature of what they were doing; judging from the solemnity of their expressions, he might have been a corpse.

"Now, look here—" Mike began only to stop abruptly.

He felt waves of dizziness assailing him, staggered and put a hand on the back of the chair to try to save himself from falling. The face of the undertaker appeared to be going round in circles, moving more and more rapidly. He felt his senses failing and tried to fight against it, but he did not lose consciousness completely for some minutes. He felt himself being lifted bodily and put into the coffin. He felt them fold his arms across his breast, and tuck his clothes in. He heard the lid drop down, and everything was dark. He tried to shout, but no sound came. He tried to struggle, but could not move. He was gripped in a horror which made him feel icy cold, yet he knew he was sweating.

Then he lost consciousness.

After a few days Gordon Craigie had deliberately taken Mark Errol off the Edgware Road "beat," because he did not think it was helping Mark any to be too close to the scene of his cousin's last appearance. He was glad he had done so when the younger agent who had taken his place telephoned to report, and, an hour later— just after eleven o'clock that morning—the young agent talked to Bill Loftus in the smoking-room of the Carilon Club. He spoke in undertones.

"That's all I can tell you, Bill. The hearse came up with one other car. They were inside for about half an hour, then they came out and pushed the coffin into the hearse. Two or three people left the house and got into the second car. I didn't follow—I left that to Pip. I haven't been in the house—do you think I ought to have a look inside?"

"We're both going to now," said Loftus.

He telephoned the office before he went, and Craigie's voice held a hint of excitement. Craigie had received a telephone call from Pip Evans, a youthful agent of considerable resource, who had also been near the Edgware Road house. The funeral party had gone to the crematorium at Golders Green. The coffin had been taken out, and was on the way to the chapel, but Evans had stopped the service. At the first hitch, the "mourners" had left and hurried off, but the undertaker and his men, protesting that they knew nothing about any trouble, remained. The crematorium authorities had been helpful, but naturally wanted authority for stopping the cremation; would Craigie arrange it with the police, Loftus asked.

"I telephoned Miller at the Yard and asked him to tell the people there to expect you, and that you have full police authority for the occasion," Craigie said. "Don't worry about the Edgware Road house; I'll look after that now."

"All right," said Loftus heavily.

"Telephone me again as soon as you can," said Craigie.

Each knew what was in the other's mind. Neither thought seriously that they would find anything but Mike's body. Neither of them worried about how it had been done, nor how the undertakers had been dealt with; they were acutely conscious of the fact that Mike had been allowed to stay at the house without any effort being made to get him away.

At the crematorium Loftus got out of the car stiffly and went to the office. The coffin, which was still fastened down, was in the morgue. The air of the place was cold and Loftus shivered as he approached the coffin with the secretary. His companion, Merton, stayed outside.

"I'm glad you've come," said the secretary, a little anxiously. "Naturally, I stopped everything when there was any suggestion of mystery, but it's a remarkable business."

"Where is the hearse?" asked Loftus.

"Still outside," said the secretary. "I sent it away from the main entrance, so you probably didn't see it."

"I didn't," said Loftus.

He still felt grim, and hated the thought of what he would see when the coffin was opened. He watched a man unscrewing the lid, and the fellow seemed to take an unconscionable time about it, but at last all the screws were out, and the man lifted the lid.

Inside were a few bricks, some dirt and gravel and a lining of old newspapers.

7

THE CURIOUS BEHAVIOUR OF AN UNDERTAKER

Loftus stared down at the rubbish for what seemed a long time, and then began to grin. He looked up into the secretary's startled face, and, unable to help himself, he laughed aloud.

"Beautiful!" he exclaimed. "Perfect! Where's your telephone?"

The secretary was a sensible man, who raised no question but led Loftus to his office. Loftus telephoned Craigie and reported joyfully, looking out of the window as he did so. The hearse was in view, with the undertaker and his two assistants standing by it, all of them looking disconsolate and alarmed. It occurred to Loftus that they had been cunningly deceived, but he was concerned with nothing so much as the fact that Mike was not dead; Brenn would not have gone to such lengths to make it appear as if he were unless he were alive.

The undertaker moved to the front of the hearse, and climbed in, while Loftus went on talking to Craigie. The two undertaker's assistants were lounging by the open doors at the back of the hearse—until suddenly the engine started up, the two men jumped in, and the hearse, already facing towards the gates, moved off at a startling pace.

He roared: "They're going, Gordon!" and banged the receiver down, jumping to his feet. It was in such moments that his leg failed him—and he tripped up and fell against the desk. The secretary had run out of the room the moment he had seen what was happening, but he reached the drive as the hearse disappeared, and Merton joined him.

Loftus recovered his balance and stared gloomily out of the window. He was more puzzled than angry, for he could not understand why the undertaker had left it so long before making a getaway. Now it was certain that he was involved in the trickery; perhaps he had hoped to evade suspicion, and at the last moment something had made him change his mind.

He picked up the telephone and called Craigie again, gave him the number of the hearse, and suggested that a police search be made for it. He was not surprised when he was back at the office an hour later to learn that the hearse had been found at the side of a road leading out of London in the Hertford direction, nor that both hearse and private car had been stolen earlier that day from a garage in South London. The genuine undertaker was in bed, ill, and it was a lock-up garage.

"And so," said Loftus, sitting back in his chair, "we've discovered that Brenn has a nice sense of the macabre."

Craigie said: "Yes. They wanted us to think Mike was dead, of course."

"It's a safe bet that he's alive," said Loftus, beaming. "Taken by and large, that's all that matters, isn't it?"

"We've lost track of Mike," Craigie said. "What ideas have you about that?"

Loftus pulled at his upper lip.

"If you must have some, what about this: since Brenn identified

Carruthers last night as the man whom he had brought from Woking on the day Mike was shot, he knew that the house was being watched. To get Mike away he adopted this method—and you know, had that coffin been burned we would have written Mike off. So would his friends and relatives; we would have had to advise them. Brenn is very deep."

"I wish I saw *why* he went to such lengths," said Craigie.

"I also wish we could see through the mists," said Loftus, who remained in high fettle. "After that shock, I don't mind what crops up in the next day or two! You've got the police busy searching the districts through which the hearse and the car passed, I suppose."

"Yes."

"And nothing else has come in?"

"Nothing at all," said Craigie, "nothing at all. If there isn't a development soon we shall probably have to ease up, Bill. The unsolved mystery of the four blind professors." He smiled without humour. "There's something we've missed," he said, "something that's obvious but evades us. Everything leads to a dead end. We may have scared Brenn into keeping quiet for a little while, but I can't believe that is the only explanation of his going to earth."

A green light glowed on the mantelpiece. It always showed when anyone outside wanted to come in, for the door of the office was a sliding one, and people who entered the building had no idea that it was there unless they were initiated. There were several lights, one used by regular agents, one used by Loftus and Hammond, and a third used by the few people outside the Department who had the right of entry at any time.

This was the third light.

Craigie leaned forward and pressed a bell-push, and the door slid open. A man strode into the room, thick-set, powerful of shoulders, and with a pale, round face.

"Don't get up," said the Rt. Hon. Graham Hershall, as Craigie started to rise, and the door closed behind him. "Well, Craigie, what have you got to tell me?"

Craigie stood by the mantelpiece, and the Prime Minister perched himself on the arm of the chair, then took out a cigarcase. Both of the others were smoking, and he lit up.

"Practically nothing new," said Craigie. "The other six members of the Commission are still quite fit, and there has been nothing to suggest that anyone is attempting to injure them. We've had more bother with the man who calls himself Brenn—you probably remember him?"

"I do," said Hershall.

"We can't say for sure that he is responsible for what happened to Hartley," went on Craigie. "We only know that he claims to be working in opposition to a man named Mandino, which is all very melodramatic, I'm afraid, sir. In fact—" he paused.

"Go on," said Hershall.

"A thought has just occurred to me," said Craigie, frowning. "Everything that's been done has the look of being a deliberate red-herring. Even the fact that Brenn has, in effect, challenged us to do him any injury suggests that he might be trying to draw off attention from someone else. I haven't given that serious consideration. If it's the explanation, then he's being successful!"

"I suppose so," said the Prime Minister.

It occurred to neither of the men to ask why he had come, for it was his habit to slip into the office rather than to telephone. He admitted to a few of his close friends that he had a soft spot for Department "Z" and all its members, especially Loftus and Craigie. He had been instrumental in saving them from the axe on more than one occasion, and when he heard criticism of the Department he stamped on it heavily. Since he had become Prime Minister the work of the Department had been much more easily carried on.

"Increase your pressure," Hershall went on, "I don't like the mystery. I don't like anything about it—and especially do I dislike the fact that Professor Gilbert Parmitter, who has been working in Aden for some time in connection with Middle East oil supplies, was stricken by blindness yesterday. I had the information an hour ago. I'll leave it to you to find out what you can about things out there, Craigie. Now I must be off!"

He nodded, and turned to the wall. Craigie only just had the presence of mind to press the button which opened the door, and he watched Hershall go out and heard him stamping down the stairs.

"There are times when we just can't see for looking," said Loftus in some excitement. "We know that this irritant is usually introduced through an eye lotion, or a similar preparation which has been tampered with. We haven't found what it is, and we haven't found a cure."

"That isn't our pigeon," Craigie said, "and it's being worked on."

"Yes, but we've been fiddling about trying to prevent it from being used on others, and we've been holding our hand—we should have collared that man Witherspoon. We knew that he might be a doctor. I mean, someone *invented* this stuff!"

"I don't see that we could have done much more than we have, whatever we are looking for," said Craigie. "You may be right about Witherspoon, though. I suppose you want to go to see him?"

"Yes. What about the Edgware Road house?"

"It was empty, and everything which might have helped us was removed. It's under lease to a man now in India, and whose wife and family went out with him—agents sub-let it to a man calling himself Crow. That is, to Brenn. But you know all that," went on Craigie. "Don't be too rough with Witherspoon, even if you see him."

"That's the trouble," said Loftus. "I expect he'll be gone."

Although he was at Witherspoon's Kensington flat within half an hour he was too late. The place was empty and locked up. There were dust-sheets over the furniture, so obviously Witherspoon expected to be away for some time. He had left no forwarding address at the post office, and there was nothing at all in the flat to give any clue as to his whereabouts or the work on which he was engaged. The agent who had been watching him had not seen him go.

Later that day, Loftus, Hammond and Craigie were at the office, none of them particularly talkative. A blank seemed to have been drawn in every possible direction. It seemed more likely than ever that they had been lured into concentrating on Brenn while something else, of greater importance, was going on. The thought grew more disturbing when, within half an hour of each other, two messages came in: Lord Daggon, millionaire ship-owner, who had assisted the Commission but had not been a member of it, had lost his sight, and Sir Andrew McGilly, Chairman of the Board of the London-Suburban Building Society, who had rendered much assistance to the Commission, was also afflicted.

Even the most reactionary members of Whitehall began to get worried.

The man who called himself Brenn, or Crow, whichever took his fancy at the moment, entered a large house on the outskirts of St. Albans, and immediately went upstairs. The door had been opened by a soft-footed little maid, and from one of the rooms Henry's nervous face appeared.

"Is everything all right, Mr. Brenn?" he asked.

"Everything is perfectly all right!" declared Brenn, jovially.

"We have them guessing wildly, Henry—it could hardly be better! Once upon a time I would have been alarmed by Craigie's interest, but I have come to the conclusion that he has been greatly over-rated."

Brenn washed, had a good dinner which Bessie served, and then, smoking a small cigar, he went upstairs to a large, airy room on the second floor. The house, of Georgian design, was planned on straightforward lines, and its spaciousness was aided by its high ceilings.

Mike Errol was sitting in an easy-chair, with a book open on his knee. He put it down quickly when he saw Brenn.

"Good evening!" greeted Brenn, genially, and rubbed his hands together. "I do wish I could have seen you before, Errol, but I have been very busy; I just haven't had time. Sit down, sit down, my friend! Now, tell me—how are you?"

"If I don't get some fresh air I shall peg out," said Mike sharply.

"Oh, I don't think it will be as bad as that," said Brenn. "You are a very resilient young man, and subject to one or two little things, you will be able to stroll in the grounds tomorrow, and every day until you have fully recovered."

"It's about time," Mike grunted.

He felt weaker than ever and still affected by the nightmare memory of being screwed into the coffin. He had no idea of what had happened subsequently, but he suspected that it had been a ruse to get him away from London without serious difficulty. He had not come round until he was in this room, and he felt no after-effects.

"I shouldn't adopt that attitude, Errol, if I were you," said Brenn. "You are not a free agent, remember; you are working for me. Or is it for Craigie?" he added, swiftly.

Something about his expression made Mike suspicious of what was coming, and so he controlled his features and stared at the man bewilderedly.

"Who *is* this Craigie who worries you so much?"

"He doesn't worry me at all," said Brenn quickly. "When did you last see Loftus?"

"Loftus?" echoed Mike, blankly.

This attempt to get the truth from him could not have been timed more perfectly. His head was aching and he felt numbed. If Brenn exerted physical pressure he did not think that he would be able to withstand it, but he composed his features and returned the man's gaze.

"I think you would know Loftus if you worked for Craigie," Brenn said at last. "Now, Errol, I have been making one or two inquiries about you. You see a lot of your cousin, don't you?"

"Mark? Yes."

"What does *he* do for a living?"

"He doesn't need to do anything. He's wealthy."

"He is a young man, physically fit, not a playboy, and with no particular hobbies," said Brenn. "So are you—that is why I am doubtful about you."

"What are you driving at?" Mike stood up and paced the room, perspiring freely.

"I just want to make sure of you," said Brenn softly. "I cannot afford to take chances, but I am beginning to think that you are just the man I was looking for, especially in view of your knowledge of Julia Hartley. What does your own fiancée think about you dancing attendance on Julia?" added Brenn. The words jolted Mike, and made him realise how thoroughly Brenn was working. It also made him search his mind anxiously lest he had done anything which Brenn might discover, to prove that he worked for Craigie. He had been so careful that he did not think it really likely. Yet he had a feeling that Brenn was playing a cat-and-mouse game with him.

"Let's keep her name out of this," he said, coldly.

"I see—Miss Brent would not approve! And you are fond of her, of course, very fond of her. Really, you are a most foolish and reckless young man, Errol, but you will do excellently for my purpose."

"What *is* your purpose?"

"When you have had a week or two of convalescence, and my other doubts have been dispelled, I will tell you," said Brenn. "After all, *you* were trying something on your own, weren't you? Or was that a bluff?"

"Please yourself," said Mike, as perfunctorily as he could. "What I was doing is my business. If we work together we might compare notes, but not until we do."

He knew the words were foolish as soon as he had uttered them— and when he saw Brenn's change of expression he backed away, for the man had suddenly become malignant, all the geniality faded from his face.

He took a step towards Mike; then another.

He held one hand in front of him, the fingers crooked like a great claw. He advanced again very slowly, and his gaze did not turn away from Mike, who stood quite still after his first involuntary movement, and tried to brazen it out.

"Listen to me, Errol," said Brenn in a harsh voice, "you will work for me and you will tell me what I want to know. You were trying to blackmail Hartley. Admit it! You have something on him, and you were trying to blackmail him! That's the truth—admit it, and—*tell me what you know about the gentleman!*"

8

NEW VICTIMS

Had Mike been his normal self he would have had no difficulty in answering with something both evasive and mysterious; possessed of sufficient poise, he could have carried it off. Instead, with Brenn's blazing amber eyes only a foot away from him, Mike just stared back without speaking. His legs were beginning to tremble and his knees felt weak. Brenn believed that he had something on Hartley; what could he think up, on the spur of the moment, that would be convincing? He recalled what he had said at Woking, every sentence was clearly etched on his mind. He had bluffed, in spite of his wound, and committed himself to nothing. Brenn had asked what he wanted of Hartley and he had replied: "You ought to know." In the interval he had racked his brains to find some plausible story, but now Brenn's sudden attack caught him unprepared.

Brenn struck him on the face.

The blow was light, but it was strong enough to send Mike reeling backwards. His legs struck against his chair and he sank into it.

Then, from some dim recesses of his mind, there came an idea.

Brenn thought that he could blackmail Hartley.

Brenn wanted to know what he was supposed to know.

Brenn would not do him serious injury until he had learned what it was.

His breath was short and his words came in gasps.

"If you think—that's going—to help you—you're—wrong!" He forced himself to return the other's gaze as Brenn drew nearer and peered down. The change in the man was remarkable and yet Mike had a feeling that it was all deliberately engineered, an old trick which he was using again to try to be impressive.

Brenn stood back.

"Is it blackmail?" His voice was more composed.

"Yes," said Mike.

"Listen to me, Errol. I don't know what you think I am, but I give you this warning. If you try to hold out on me you will suffer for it very much indeed. I am a patient man and I am in no great hurry, but I intend to know what you can tell me about the Hartleys before you are allowed to get in touch with them again. Don't make any mistake about that."

He turned and went out.

Mike wiped the perspiration from his forehead. He felt so weak that his body was trembling, and his hands would not keep still. It was hardly credible that Brenn had gone away at such a moment. A little more pressure, and he must have realised the truth. Perhaps he felt so certain of getting what he wanted that he preferred to pile on the suspense.

After a while Mike felt better.

What he wanted was a plausible "reason" for being able to black-mail Hartley, but his mind would not work smoothly enough to present one. If Loftus or Hammond were in his position their more agile minds would have little difficulty, but he had been pitchforked into a situation which he was not really capable of handling. He was not even sure that he had done the best possible thing so far; the lack of knowledge of what was going on outside was getting on his nerves, too. They—the Department—must have known where he was in the Edgware Road, as Carruthers had made the journey with him, yet they had left him severely alone.

From that he had judged that they wanted him to work with Brenn. Of course they did, that was an obvious move. But now they would think him dead. Regina would probably be told that he was dead. The coffin—*what had happened while he had been unconscious in the coffin?* What brilliant trick had Brenn played?

He found himself beginning to feel really afraid of Brenn.

Next day, when the sun had warmed the early morning mist and the first tints of autumn were showing in the leaves of the trees, he was allowed into the garden of the house. It was surrounded by a high wall on three sides, and by a thick hedge on the other. There was a gate to the drive from this walled garden and it was locked. One of the men who had been with the undertaker watched him as he walked lazily about the grounds, letting the sun soak into him. After a while he went to a garden-seat and sat in the shade. His chief thought was of the fresh air and the illusion of freedom that it gave him. If he could get mentally and physically strong he would be better able to cope.

He lay back and closed his eyes.

A shadow fell upon him, but he was not aware of it until, after a few minutes of pleasant drowsiness, when he was between sleeping and waking, he grew conscious of someone standing and staring at him. He did not know what made him aware of it; one moment he had his eyes closed, the next he opened them and sat up abruptly.

"Good morning!" a woman said.

Mike blinked, for he had never seen her before. She was dressed in a flowered frock and wore a floppy hat, which kept the sun out of her eyes, but not off the lower part of her face. She was smiling, and she was good to look upon.

"Oh—er—hallo," said Mike, beginning to struggle to his feet.

"Please don't get up," she said. She smiled and moved forward, sitting down next to him and turning so that she could see him easily. "Are you feeling better?"

"Oh, much," said Mike.

"I am so glad." She had a curious voice. It was pleasant and yet almost monotonous, and her gaze seemed disturbed. She seemed to be thinking of something else, although she kept looking at him. It was another trick on Brenn's part, of course, and this time an old one. Mike felt wary, yet he did not feel that he was strong enough to match his wits with anyone.

"How long have you been here?" she asked.

"Oh—only a day," said Mike, startled.

"Only a day—how lucky you are! What is your name?"

"Errol—Mike Errol."

"Mike for Michael, I suppose," she said, and for the first time it occurred to him that she might be simple-minded. Her words had a childish quality, and there was something about her expression, a quality of sadness, which affected him oddly, although he tried to tell himself that it was all part of the trick.

She leaned forward. "Is that man near by?"

"Which man?"

"The man who was watching. He was behind the trees in the corner by the roses—ah! I can see from your expression that he is still there."

"He is, yes," said Mike, "but he can't hear us."

"Oh, don't be silly," she said, "they can hear everything and see everything. *Everything!* Sometimes I think I will go mad if I don't get away from here, but—they won't let me go." Her expression grew piteous. "They just won't let me go, and I can't do anything about it. I can't do anything at all."

"Surely—" began Mike.

"*Shhh!* I mustn't talk too much about it; they don't like me to." She made an obvious effort to regain her self-control, and sent him a tremulous smile. "After all, they treat me very well, and I have plenty to eat and drink and to read; that's the most important thing, isn't it? I suppose the rest doesn't matter really." She stared for some seconds, while Mike tried not to show his feelings, and then she leaned forward and gripped his hand. Hers was icy cold; she startled him. "Mr. Errol! Are you going out of here?"

"I hope to," said Mike.

"If you do, tell my father that—" She broke off abruptly.

It was one of the most eerie things Mike had experienced. She stared past him towards the wall, her face set into a mask of horror. He turned abruptly and saw Brenn coming towards them. It was almost as if Brenn had heard what she had said and chosen that moment to interrupt.

"No!" she said, in a strangled voice, "*no!*"

Brenn drew up and smiled at her.

"Hallo, Pamela—are you enjoying your talk?"

"No," she said. "No, I *hate* him, he's a beast! Yes, you are!" she snapped, turning on Mike, "an utter beast, or you wouldn't talk to me like that!" She stood up abruptly and hurried away, and the man who had been watching opened the door in the wall for her. Mike watched her disappear, then turned and looked up into Brenn's smiling face.

"Poor Pamela," said Brenn softly. "She suffers from delusions, and yet it isn't so long since she was a really normal, happy woman. She was carrying a child and met with an accident. The child was born prematurely and died, and it turned her mind. I have been looking after her for a long time—you see how philanthropical I am! Dr. Witherspoon has hopes of her recovery, I think."

"Who is she?" asked Mike with an effort.

"A woman who is alone in the world—widowed," said Brenn. "I knew the husband slightly, and I have always felt responsible for her. Well, Errol—what about the thing we were discussing last night? Are you prepared to tell me what you have on Hartley?"

"Not yet," said Mike quietly.

Brenn shrugged, and sat down beside him, taking out a pipe

and filling it. A gentle breeze cooled the air and made the leaves of the trees rustle and whisper, an occasional bird flitted across the garden, and wasps and bees hummed about the flowers. It was all so pleasant and natural on the surface—and Brenn might have been a genial host, arguing tolerantly with a young man who lacked his experience.

"You mustn't be so obstinate," he said. "It won't do you any good. You lied to me at Woking, didn't you?"

Mike said nothing.

"Perhaps it wasn't a direct lie, but one was implied," said Brenn. "You told me that Hartley had been taken ill; actually, you knew that he had gone blind, didn't you?"

Mike said: "Yes."

"Why did you lie about it?"

"There was no question of lying," said Mike. "I called it an illness, which it was, and you didn't press for details."

"No, that's true," admitted Brenn, lighting his pipe and drawing at it with every appearance of satisfaction. "But little things like that are instructive, you know. Actually, *I* am responsible for Hartley's blindness."

"Oh," said Mike, blankly.

"It was not difficult to arrange," went on Brenn, "and it served my purpose. It's a curious weapon, isn't it?" He puffed at his pipe and smiled at Mike benignly. "I find it very useful. Can you imagine what it is like, Errol, not to be able to see? To find yourself, suddenly and with hardly any warning—except a little irritation at the eyes and a little confused vision under strain—cut off from all visible things. Look about this garden, for instance. Beautiful! Imagine what it is like to wake up one day and to realise that you will *never* be able to see again."

Mike said nothing; his throat was constricted and his breathing laboured.

"It is very sad," said Brenn, "but—well, if you *are* obstinate I shall have to treat you."

He stood up and walked sharply away.

Mike remained staring after him, the delight of the sunny morning and the cool wind and the fresh air all gone. It was some time before he stood up and walked about the garden again—and everything he saw took on an added beauty.

Unknown to Mike Errol, there were three more victims of blindness that day. A Permanent Under-Secretary to the Ministry of Works was stricken soon after mid-day. One of the staff of the six members of the mission was a second victim. The third was Professor Leslie Miles, a prominent economist, who was to have been consulted by the Commission within a few days.

Craigie, Loftus and Hammond sat together in the office at Whitehall. It was seldom that all of them looked so downcast and seldom that they were so affected by a case that, between them, they could not find a smile or a quip. They had been through all the reports which had come in, and discussed them, their voices sober and their expressions sombre.

Loftus broke the silence.

"It looks to me, Gordon, as if we've reached the end of the 'go slow' phase. We've got to find out what we can. Fergus Grey might give us something, and Julia must be more closely questioned. We can't just sit back and await events any longer; we've done it for too long."

Craigie looked at Hammond.

"What do you think, Bruce?"

Hammond said: "I'm inclined to agree with Bill, but I don't see that there's a lot we can do, even if we tackle Grey. By waiting long enough to let Brenn take Mike away, and for Witherspoon to disappear, we've spiked our own guns. The sum total of what we know, after over three weeks working, is that many people are going down with this blindness. They appear to be all connected with the Commission, but I don't know that we can take that for granted. I mean"—he stirred in his chair and went on slowly—"all those we've heard about are connected with it in some way or other, but there may be victims of whom we haven't yet heard."

"Need we assume that?" asked Loftus.

"We've got to take it into account as a possibility," said Hammond, quietly. "At the moment we haven't even an inkling of what is behind it all. It might be an attempt to delay the findings of the Commission, but I'm not convinced of that."

"You mean that if one Commission failed, another would be set up," said Craigie, drawing at his pipe. "That's right enough. This working in the dark is worrying," he went on, "but I don't see that we're going to improve the position by tackling Grey or Julia Hartley yet. When all's said and done, everything really depends on word from Mike. If we can find him and if we can trace Brenn again, then I'd say let's raid the place and be done with it. I think we made a mistake in keeping away from the Edgware Road house, but we weren't to know that."

"We haven't got the right angle at all," Loftus said.

"That's partly true," said Craigie, "and I think it's probable that we weren't intended to get the right angle."

Loftus stood up, and walked slowly across the room. His big figure looked fat, his clothes fitted him badly, and his hair was dishevelled.

"You mean that they're putting it across us properly? I wouldn't be surprised if you're right. If you could suggest only one little thing to do, just one possibility, I'd feel happier. That's why I'm in favour of going for Fergus Grey, I suppose. As you're both really against it, I withdraw the suggestion!"

"We'll wait for Mike a few more days," Craigie said.

"Right," said Loftus. "Meanwhile, what's doing? All our people and all the police are keeping an eye open for Witherspoon and Brenn, not to mention Henry. Is that the limit?"

"Very nearly," admitted Craigie. "I—"

He broke off as the telephone rang. He heard the operator say: "Press Button A," and then heard Carruthers' voice. Carruthers began to spell his name backwards, and Craigie said quickly:

"All right—carry on."

Carruthers said: "Gordon, what shall I do? Upstairs, talking to Martha Dale, there's a man who looks for all the world like Witherspoon—he wants a room at the Guest House. Shall I tell Martha to say 'yes'?"

9

DR. WITHERSPOON COMES TO STAY

"Yes," said Craigie, without hesitation.

"Thanks," said Carruthers. "I'll call you again soon."

In the cupboard under the stairs at the Guest House he replaced the receiver and smoothed down his hair before stepping into the hall. Jim Dale was looking at him from the landing, and Carruthers nodded. Dale disappeared, and Martha's voice, alternating with the quiet voice of the man who looked like Witherspoon, sounded clearly through the house.

Carruthers regarded the front door in some bewilderment.

Of all the things he had expected, this was the last. He had not seen Witherspoon himself, but he had the description which Craigie had circulated, and he had little doubt that it was the same man. When it came to asking himself why a colleague of Brenn's should deliberately come to the Woking house he could think of no answer. It was in character with the rest of the crazy affair, and Carruthers preferred those which were more straightforward.

He heard footsteps on the stairs. Martha was seeing the visitor out.

"Good-day, Mrs. Dale," said Witherspoon.

He left the house, and Carruthers, who had taken cover in the lounge, stepped into the hall. Dale came haltingly down the stairs and Martha looked at Carruthers with some excitement.

"*Is* it this awful rogue of yours, Carry?"

"I don't think there's much doubt," said Carruthers, slowly, "but if you ask me why—I give up!"

"Can't you tell us anything more, old man?" asked Dale.

"I wish I could," said Carruthers, "but the truth is I know next to nothing; it's the most hopeless mix-up I've ever struck, and I've met a few. Er—you know there might be a spot or two of trouble again, don't you?"

"I've assumed that it's not impossible," said Dale, dryly. "We're not worried about that, but we would like some idea of what's going to happen."

"And wouldn't I!" exclaimed Carruthers.

"I suppose the fellow will come," said Dale.

"I can't see any reason why he should book a room unless he intends to use it," said Carruthers. He looked out of the window towards the common, where he could see Witherspoon's tall, angular figure, now nearly half a mile away; he also saw the man who was following him—none other than Pip Evans, who had reported the arrival of the hearse at Edgware Road; and who had been on duty near the Guest House. The two men disappeared and Carruthers went on with satisfaction: "Well, I don't think he'll get away, anyhow."

Pip Evans followed Witherspoon as far as Waterloo, and then to Piccadilly. At the station there, Mecca of those who wished to evade anyone who followed them, Witherspoon contrived to lose him. Disconsolately Pip reported to Craigie.

On the following afternoon, about three o'clock, Mr.—or Dr.— Witherspoon arrived at the Guest House. He came by taxi from the station, and his luggage included two cabin trunks and four large pig-skin suitcases. He apologised for the amount of luggage, and said that he had a great deal of work to do.

For three days Witherspoon was a model guest. He was punctual at meals, he made no noise, and he had no special requests. He spent most of the time in his room, but whenever he went out he locked his door. The elementary lock was no obstacle to Carruthers, who went through his room three times in those three days, but found nothing at all of interest except a microscope and several slides, which he did not touch. Judging from his books, Witherspoon was an anthropologist, but he possessed nothing to suggest that he had medical degrees.

On the fourth day he had a visitor. Carruthers began to sit up and take notice, for the visitor was Julia Hartley.

Carruthers heard her go up to his room, with Martha chattering at her side. Witherspoon greeted her courteously, firmly disposed of Martha, took Julia in, and locked the door. Carruthers hurried up to the landing.

He heard every word that followed.

There had been moments in the past few weeks when Julia Hartley had felt that she could not carry on. The sight of her father made her want to cry. The work which his affliction put on her shoulders worried her far less than the knowledge that he was so helpless. Physically he was as well as ever, but there was no indication that he would recover his sight.

She had been approached by Bruce Hammond and told frankly what the Department wanted. It was possible that some effort would be made by persons unknown to her to question her as well as her father. If she were questioned about Mike Errol she was to say only that he was an acquaintance who had pressed his attentions, but had suddenly disappeared. She was at liberty to say what she liked about Bruce Hammond and others of the Department men, provided she repeated whatever conversation ensued.

An hour before she had come to the Guest House, Mrs. McFarlane had called her to the telephone. The handy-man, Forbeson, had been hovering near, but the talking had been done mostly by the man at the other end of the line.

What he had said, Carruthers gathered from Julia's opening remarks.

She sat in an easy-chair and Witherspoon sat at a small table, on which was his microscope. His heavy-lidded eyes were narrowed and his parchment-like face seemed unnatural.

"I am very glad to see you so soon, Miss Hartley."

"I received a telephone call suggesting that you would be able to help my father," said Julia in a strained voice. "Is that right?"

"I think perhaps I can be of assistance," said Witherspoon, "subject to certain conditions."

"What are they?" demanded Julia.

"They are very simple," Witherspoon assured her. "You will be able to carry out the treatment yourself, it is so easy. I will instruct you from day to day. You will say nothing at all to the man Hammond, who is a frequent visitor—as you probably know, he is a member of a Secret Service Department."

Julia said: "I did not know anything of the kind!"

"Indeed?" asked Witherspoon. "Then what excuse has he offered for his frequent attendances?"

"He says he is a Government official connected with the Commission on which my father was sitting," said Julia. "Are you serious?"

Witherspoon said: "My dear Miss Hartley, I do not talk for the sake of it. Hammond is a member of a Department which calls itself secret. He may or may not have deceived you. I think there are others taking an interest in your father's affliction. The point which I have to make is—if any of them so much as suspects that he is being treated, the treatment will stop forthwith."

Julia said nothing.

Outside, Carruthers looked at the door.

"I perceive that you are a woman of intelligence," went on Witherspoon, gently. "The interest which these people have in your father is not welcome to me or to my friends. We can, and will, restore your father's sight subject to your willing co-operation with us. On the slightest hint that you are not co-operating, I repeat, the treatment will cease. And there are one or two questions I have to ask you. You are acquainted with a man named Errol, Michael Errol."

"Yes," said Julia.

"Did he explain *why* he forced himself upon you?"

Carruthers did not think that Julia knew that she was being over-heard, and if she were loyal she would clear Mike of suspicion, but the cunning of the approach worried him. The bait was her father's recovery; no girl could be blamed for refusing to try to make sure of that.

"He was"—she shrugged—"an admirer of mine."

"Just that?"

"*I* don't know!" She flared up again, and jumped from her chair. "I thought he was sincere when he said that he—he was in love with me, but for all I know he might have caused my father's blindness! Do you know him?"

"Fairly well," said Witherspoon. "Or shall we say that I did know him?" There was a hint of laughter in his voice, and Carruthers was comparing his words and the way in which he uttered them with Brenn's manner. They were so alike—the same men might have been talking.

"What do you mean?" flashed Julia.

"I came across Mr. Errol in curious circumstances, but he has moved on," said Witherspoon. "Now, Miss Hartley—what kind of questions does Hammond ask you?"

"I don't understand you. He comes to get information from my father, and I give it to him." Her voice hardened suddenly. "If you are trying to get information from me about the Commission you can stop trying."

"Even at the cost of your father's sight?" asked Witherspoon, softly. Then he went on: "But I do not particularly want such information,

Miss Hartley, I am merely emphasising the fact that, to ensure his recovery, you will have to do exactly what I say. *Only* I can effect a cure."

Abruptly, she said:

"All right. What have I to do?"

"I will post you a little lotion, which you will use to bathe his eyes to-morrow morning, to-morrow afternoon, and before he goes to bed at night," said Witherspoon. "The effect will not be instantaneous, but you will hardly expect that, will you? Two days later you will receive a second lotion. You will use that in exactly the same way. Then I will send for you again." He stood up and extended his hand. "Good-day, Miss Hartley."

Carruthers hurried into his room.

Julia left the other room and walked down the stairs, and Witherspoon stood watching her. His door and the front door closed simultaneously, and for a while the house was very quiet.

Carruthers telephoned Craigie: Julia had carried out her promise, Witherspoon had been assured that she did not know that Mike worked for the Department, but he had implied that Mike was dead. Carruthers admitted that he could not make head or tail of it.

"You're not alone in that," said Craigie. "Try to find out what he sends to Hartley. If it does his eyes any good we might be able to get supplies of it from somewhere else."

"All right," said Carruthers, "but—" He broke off.

"Go on," said Craigie.

"It's so absurd!" exclaimed Carruthers. "Brenn knows that I'm here and Witherspoon must know that I probably overheard every word. It just doesn't tie-up."

"I think it does," said Craigie, quietly.

He passed the news on to Loftus, who agreed that it did tie-up.

"Of course, Witherspoon wanted us to hear what he said to Julia; he wants us to know that he has—or claims to have—a cure for the blindness." He stood quite still, his large features set in a wooden expression, and then he added softly: "Gordon, I think something is dawning."

"We had to have a break sooner or later," said Craigie.

"Of course, you've got it, too. Witherspoon has told us that he can put Hartley right. If he can do that to Hartley, then he can cure the others. In short—"

"Witherspoon says: 'Hands off me,'" said Craigie. "Yes, that's it, Bill. He's had the effrontery to go to the Guest House; he's made it clear that if anything happens to him there's no help for Hartley *or* the others. In other words—"

"He has us by the short hairs," said Loftus. "You know, I'm beginning to admire this bunch!"

"I'm beginning to get really worried by them," said Craigie. "I think—*confound* that telephone!"

A little light was glowing in one of the instruments—the indoor telephone. It was a porter to say that there had been a letter left by hand marked *"Urgent and Important."*

"I'll send for it," Craigie said.

One of his whims was to allow no junior staff to enter the office, and, in fact, none of them knew just where it was. To get the message he telephoned another office and then went along to fetch it. He came back with it unopened in his hand, and Loftus watched him slit the envelope.

"Well?" said Loftus a moment later.

Craigie smiled faintly.

"Yes, they're good," he said. "Listen. 'Mr. Gabriel Witherspoon presents his compliments to Mr. Gordon Craigie, and would appreciate the favour of a visit from Mr. Craigie at the Guest House, Guildford Road, Woking, at any time. Only a personal interview will serve any useful purpose.'" He looked up, and his smile broadened. "That's all, Bill."

"So Mr. Witherspoon proposes to make it quite clear that he has us by the short hairs," said Loftus. "Do you mind if I come along?"

"No," said Craigie, "you can drive."

* * *

83

Witherspoon greeted Craigie and Loftus with no show of enthusiasm, but with his unfailing courtesy. He apologised for the untidiness of his room and for the fact that he had only one really comfortable chair, and he hoped Mr. Loftus would not mind sitting on the bed. He himself sat at the table, on a high-backed chair, and in a position from which he could see the others without turning to look at either of them.

"Isn't Mr. Carruthers going to join us," he added, without a smile. "He has worked so ardently that he surely deserves to be present?"

Craigie smiled.

"We'll tell him what you have to say afterwards."

"As you please," said Witherspoon. "Now—you presumably understood from what Carruthers told you of my message to Miss Hartley that I am in a position to correct the unfortunate eye trouble which has afflicted her father?"

"Yes," said Craigie. "Her father and many others."

"I have discovered, after many years of endeavour, a substance which will induce blindness. Some quantities of this substance are in the hands of other people—I mention Brenn, for one, but there are several. While I am free and able to work with them they will use it under my direction, but if anything should happen to me—" he shrugged. "I cannot be responsible for what they might do with it. I certainly cannot cure the affliction unless I have the necessary facilities and the inclination. I hope you understand me?"

Craigie spoke quietly.

"You're trying to say that unless we give you a free hand you will let Brenn and the others use it recklessly, and you will not supply us with the cure."

"That is *exactly* what I mean," said Witherspoon. "Now, you have gone to a great deal of trouble to find out what it is all about. You might succeed. But if you do it will be disastrous for many eminent people in this country and abroad. I do not propose to allow you to interfere too much, and I am giving you this warning. My advice to you, Mr. Craigie, is to return to London, to tell your superiors that you can do nothing more—relate the details of this interview, if you think it advisable—and then allow me and my friends to work as we think fit. I can hardly make my attitude clearer, can I?"

"No," said Craigie.

"Excellent! I hope you will take my advice. I earnestly implore you *not* to imagine that you can get round this: you cannot. In good time you will understand just what I am attempting to do—and I think it shall succeed. The drug which I use is most efficacious, and can be introduced in a number of different ways—I do not need eye lotion, for instance! It gives me considerable power, as you can imagine." He sounded most good-humoured as he stood up. "In case you need a little further demonstration, I have arranged for a close friend of yours to be affected. You will doubtless hear about it shortly."

Loftus said slowly:

"Witherspoon, you're making a mistake."

"I hardly think so," said Witherspoon sharply.

"A big mistake," repeated Loftus. "I—"

There was a sharp tap on the door.

Witherspoon had locked it when the others had come in. Now he moved to the door, his gaunt, shaggy figure impressive and sinister, and turned the key.

Dale came in.

There was a curious expression on his face. He looked at Witherspoon without speaking, as if he loathed the man, and then he turned to Craigie.

"Carruthers works for you, doesn't he?"

"Yes," said Craigie.

"Come into his room, will you?" said Dale.

Something in his manner made Loftus get up from the bed too quickly, and he stumbled. Witherspoon stood looking at them without expression. Craigie and Loftus followed Dale into the next room, where Carruthers was standing by the dressing-table, staring into the mirror. They could see his reflection, his pale face, his staring eyes and the strain that was in them.

Loftus snapped: "Carry, what is it?"

Slowly, Carruthers turned round.

"I can't see," he said simply, "I just can't see."

There had been occasions in the past when Craigie had had to admit that he could see no way out of an impasse, but he had never felt so completely helpless as when he returned to Whitehall with Loftus.

The first thing Craigie did was to lift a telephone receiver and put a call in, on the private line, to Hershall. After some delay he reached the Prime Minister, and said that he would very much like to see him.

"I'll come over," said Hershall, "but it won't be for an hour."

He was punctual almost to the minute. Craigie saw the green light glow, pressed the button, and stood up as Hershall entered. His round face was not smiling; it was as if he sensed something of what they were going to say.

Craigie told him, briefly.

As he listened Hershall sat back in an easy-chair; he did not once shift his gaze, nor did he interrupt. Craigie finished, and Loftus, leaning against the mantelpiece, said slowly:

"It couldn't be much worse, sir."

"No," admitted Hershall briskly, "and yet I see advantages in the present situation. You at least know what you are up against. There's no chance that there is any measure of bluff in what the man says, I suppose?"

"I can see none," said Craigie, "except that he is probably wrong when he says that no one else can discover the cure. On the other hand, finding it might take a long time. We are in the position of knowing that if Witherspoon or Brenn wish to make *any* man blind, they can do so. I don't think the significance of that can be exaggerated."

"*Any* man," echoed Hershall, and he rubbed his eyes. "Not a happy situation at all, is it? But we can't let the fellow get away with it." When neither of the others responded, he added sharply: "Well? Can we?"

"We would like to carry on," said Craigie, toying with a pencil, "but the consequences might be very nearly disastrous. Witherspoon appears to be in a position from which he can dictate terms. Supposing, for instance, we carry on and he names any particular individual—perhaps a member of the Government. How are we to stop him from doing what he threatens?"

"So far we can't," said Hershall. "I'll have a word with one or two of the others," he went on, "and I'll telephone you soon. Meanwhile, get prepared as far as you can. They *can't* strike everyone blind." He looked at Craigie with narrowed eyes, then added quietly: "Of course, you've seen them in person, haven't you? And finding Carruthers afflicted must have been a great shock. You'll have my personal support, and you will not be blamed for anything that might go wrong."

He nodded and went out.

Loftus said: "Thank the Lord for Hershall!"

"It's just beginning to dawn on him that things might get out of hand," said Craigie. "Bill, I've never felt so near to despair as I do now. I've never felt so helpless." He rubbed his eyes, which watered a little, and then wiped them with a handkerchief. "I suppose we shall get on top of it, but—"

"Now, steady!" exhorted Loftus. "This isn't like you."

He broke off abruptly.

Craigie rubbed his eyes again, and into his face there came a peculiar expression. It was set, and his eyes seemed filled with horror—and also with incredulity. He kept staring, and Loftus stood without moving or speaking.

Slowly, Craigie said:

"Bill—move your right hand, will you?"

Loftus hesitated, and then moved his hand from his pocket to his chin. He felt inwardly cold, staring at Craigie with an increasing sense of horror. *Craigie's gaze did not follow the movement of his hand*, but kept staring towards his chest.

"Move your arm," ordered Craigie.

Loftus began: "Gordon, I—"

"Oh, it's all right," said Craigie, sharply, "it's all right! I can't see, of course, I knew I couldn't see. One moment you were standing there as large as life, then you began to get vague. Now—" he turned abruptly and groped on the table next to him for his pipe, then, still groping, he sat down heavily and began to fill it.

10

THE PLAGUE OF BLINDNESS

Craigie was persuaded to go to his flat, where a nurse was sent to him, although it was probable that he would not stay away from the office for more than a few days. Shock was the only thing which affected him, apart from the blindness, and the shock was likely to pass off before long—and the same would apply to Carruthers.

Loftus took over control at the office.

He admitted to Bruce Hammond, when Bruce came in in response to an urgent summons, that he had never felt in so hopeless a position. There was no telling from one moment to the next whether he would be able to see. Craigie had had no inkling of what had happened until the plague had smitten him.

"And it might be me next, or it might be you," Loftus said. "There isn't an answer, Bruce."

Hammond smiled soberly.

"There's an answer, and we'll find it. Have you heard from Hershall again?"

"Yes. We're to carry on as we think best."

"That means Cabinet sanction, I suppose," said Hammond, "although when you really think it out, Bill, there's nothing else we can do—we can't sit back and let Witherspoon dictate to us. Which is labouring the obvious," he added, lightly. "I know one thing we'll have to do pretty quickly."

"What's that?" asked Loftus. "I can't think."

"Both you and Gordon have been working too hard," Hammond said. "I've always thought you two get the thick end of the job. For a start, every agent who might be able to take over in emergency must know everything we know. The police should be told, too. I suggest a meeting, somewhere in secret, where you or I can talk about it. Then—" he shrugged. "As one goes down, another can take over."

Throughout London and the Home Counties members of the Department were advised by devious means, often by telephone, when some innocent-seeming message was given but which conveyed the necessary information. Members who were resting after work abroad, others who had been on the sick-list, many who were on minor tasks, and all who were assigned to the mystery of the plague of blindness, left their homes on the next day and made their way to the Renown Rooms.

They all knew the room being used, and needed to ask no questions.

For many it was the first time they had seen more than two or three other agents, and there was a buzz of conversation. Loftus, Hammond, and another old-time agent, Jim Burke, were there to receive them. Chairs were in position, and it might have been a session of any lecture. At three o'clock precisely Loftus rose from a chair on the dais and explained enough to make men look at one another and then stare incredulously towards him.

Burly Superintendent Miller, whose long, untidy moustache always looked as if it had been dusted with flour, and earned the nickname "Dusty," three inspectors, several members of the Home and Foreign Offices, were all present; and there was only the sound of Loftus' voice in the room as he went into details.

Loftus was no orator; but no crowd had ever been gripped more tightly. It was obvious on the faces of all the men and in the tenseness of their expressions.

Finally, he said:

"And that's about the lot, but I may have missed a number of points—now's the time to ask questions."

Two or three minor questions were put and answered, and there was a pause before Loftus stood up again and was about to say "That's enough," and add that instructions for every individual would be distributed within a few hours when there was a disturbance in the doorway. He saw a man opening it, and he stood very still.

Gabriel Witherspoon entered the room.

Loftus had given a word picture of him, and not a man present could have failed to know who he was. Witherspoon walked slowly and deliberately, looking neither right nor left, till he reached the dais and climbed the three steps leading to it. Then he nodded to Loftus, and turned towards the main body of the meeting. His composure was astonishing; he did not turn a hair.

Loftus did not try to stop him.

"Gentlemen," said Witherspoon in a testy voice, "I have come here to tell you that, whatever precautions you may take, you will not be able to prevent me from carrying out my intended purpose. It was foolish to bring you all here together, *because at one stroke I can deal with you all.*"

Loftus said: "Witherspoon—"

Witherspoon swung round on him.

"Be quiet, sir! I have told you often enough that you are wasting your time. You will not listen. Let it be clearly understood that every man who becomes affected by blindness in this room owes his plight *entirely* to you!"

"Ah," said Loftus. "What do you do—say *abracadabra* x-y-z? Or is there some other magic sign?"

The absurdity of the words seemed to occur to no one among the crowd. Loftus uttered them in a great effort to throw off the yoke of the man's influence.

"So it pleases you to be facetious," said Witherspoon. "Apparently I have not yet demonstrated the effect of—"

"You've demonstrated quite enough," said Loftus. The issue had been forced, and he could see only one thing to do. If he missed this chance he would be thoroughly discredited. If he allowed the others to see that Witherspoon could come and go with impunity, he would increase the man's influence tenfold. "Quite enough," he repeated. "I think it's time we took you in hand, Witherspoon, and—"

Witherspoon lifted a hand and looked towards the door.

A man was standing there, a stranger to Loftus, and he tossed something into the air. Hammond was near the door and he rushed towards the man, but he tripped over someone's foot and went sprawling. The missile, in a glass container, hit the ceiling and burst, and before Hammond could get to his feet clouds of tear gas were spreading through the room, and confusion, inevitable in any crowd, brought uproar. Loftus already choking with the gas, tried to grab Witherspoon, but the man evaded him with surprising agility, jumped down and hurried towards the door. Every man present was affected so quickly by the gas that no one could see to stop him.

When the windows were open and the uproar had subsided, and when first-aid was being given to those who were worst affected, there was no sign of Witherspoon or the man who had released the gas.

Loftus was frightened, and made no bones about admitting it. He was frightened lest there had been something more than tear gas in the fragile glass container which had been tossed into the room. He waited on tenterhooks, afraid that any of the men would report the onset of blindness. When twenty-four hours passed and no such reports were received he breathed more freely.

The next shock which he had nearly floored him. It was a message from Forbeson at Lyddon House.

Sir Basil Hartley had regained his sight.

"Now we want that lotion," Loftus said. "Forbeson's the man to get the bottle." He sent a message post haste to the odd-job man at Hartley's house, feeling that at last he had some grounds for hope.

Gabriel Witherspoon and the man who sometimes called himself Brenn were together in the house on the outskirts of St. Albans. Witherspoon was standing up in front of a desk, at which Brenn was sitting and smiling. Witherspoon's face was as blank as always, but his eyes reflected Brenn's smile.

"I think we have done very well," he said.

"Yes. What a good thing it was that we had Loftus followed, and also suspected what was going to happen when we learned what room he had gone to. And"—Brenn chuckled, in high good humour—"what a marvelous job *you* did, Witherspoon! I didn't think you would have the nerve!"

"There is little the matter with my nerve," said Witherspoon dryly. "You need not worry about that. I think that every man in the room was thoroughly scared, and I feel sure that Loftus expected them all to lose their sight. It's almost a pity that they didn't," he added, softly.

"I don't think we shall have much more trouble," said Brenn, "but if we do—" he broke off.

"We shall have to be quite ruthless," said Witherspoon. "However, we cannot complain just now. Has Pamela been in to see you to-day?"

"No," said Brenn, in a different tone. "She has been more difficult since she first met Errol. Every word they exchanged was overheard, and nothing they said can explain the change."

"There is plenty that can explain it," said Witherspoon. "The sight of another face, someone whom she did not know and who attempted to exert no influence over her, gave her a shock which had a considerable effect. It was a pity that they were allowed to meet, I think—I wish you had consulted me. However, no serious harm will come of it."

"Of course it won't," said Brenn.

In the next room Mike Errol was standing by the wall.

Only that morning he had been shifted from one room to another and he had made a discovery of great interest. He could hear practically every word which was uttered in the other room, which, he assumed, was Brenn's study. Little had been said to interest him until Witherspoon's arrival. Now he could just hear what was being said, and he stood watching tensely, still uncertain of himself, but determined that it must not be long before he made an effort to get word to Craigie.

The talk bewildered and worried him, but he gave some thought to what they said about "Pamela."

In the several days since he had seen her he had made great strides. The weather had been fine, and he had spent a lot of time out of doors. He no longer needed to cover up his wound, and although his arm was still a little stiff he could use it fairly well. When alone in his room he had massaged it and given it as much gentle exercise as he felt was wise.

As the door of the other room closed—presumably as Witherspoon went out—he frowned in concentration. Pamela was one possibility; if he could have a talk with her he might do a lot of good. During the day it would be impossible, but he believed that he knew which room she was in. It was on the next floor, immediately above his.

The rest of the day passed with agonising slowness, and the evening was almost unbearable.

The hands of the illuminated dial of his watch pointed to half-past one when eventually he pushed the clothes back and got out of bed. The house was very silent. He had heard the light switched off in the other room some time before, and he could not hear footsteps or voices. He did not dress, but went through the contents of his pockets. They had left him his penknife but that was not the tool he wanted. In the grounds he had come across a small piece of wire, which he had thrust into his pocket thinking that it might be useful some time. He found it and stepped to the door.

He worked at the lock for some time, although he took longer than was necessary to open it, because he wanted to make sure that he was not heard. At last the lock clicked back, and he waited in silence before opening the door a little.

As there was no light in the room he could not be seen, but the first thing he saw was a man sitting in an easy-chair at the head of the stairs. A small table was at his side, and on the table was a gun, a stick and a handbell. He was reading, but he glanced up from time to time, and he looked directly towards Mike.

Mike closed the door.

He was perspiring freely; the disappointment was acute, but he knew that it would be folly to go out that way. He could wait until the man left his chair for a few minutes, but he was not sure that it would be wise. After a while he brushed his hand across his forehead and grimly set about locking the door from the inside, without using the key. If he used the key the moment it was missed on the outside, an alarm would be raised. The task took him longer than it had done to force it; nearly an hour had passed before he finished and found himself in exactly the same position as when he had started.

Hardly had he finished than he saw the handle of the door turn. Straining his ears, he heard the footsteps of the guard as the man passed on a tour of inspection. He heard him go upstairs, but he was down again within a few minutes.

Mike went to the window.

The moon was shining brightly in the west and its glow spread over the garden and on the roof of a house not far away. He had the window ajar, but it was fitted with a locking device which prevented it from opening too widely, and the toughened glass could not be broken with any tool he possessed.

It was a little after half-past two.

Using his penknife, he began to work at the special fitting of the window. He believed that he could get it off and be able to replace it before the morning, but even as he worked he knew that it would be useless if the window of the girl's room was fitted with the same patent. Yet he did not slacken his efforts, and after half an hour he was able to open the window wide enough for him to get through.

He pulled on his shoes, trousers and coat, then started to climb out. There was a wide windowsill, which offered good foothold, and the drop to the garden was a short one, so that if he wished he could get down there and then climb the wall. He did not want to do that; he wanted to stay until the end, but he had to get word to Craigie; the thought had become an obsession.

He looked up, while holding on to a drain-pipe in order to keep his balance.

The pipe was likely to help him. The window above had a sill, very like his own, and if he could once reach it he would have no trouble in getting to Pamela's window. He tested his arm again. It pained him a little, but he thought it was because of stiffness more than anything else. He hauled himself up by the pipe until he was able to grip the window-sill with his sound hand.

Then he put the other up in support, and hauled himself to the next sill.

The pain in his shoulder was so great that he was afraid that he had reopened the wound. He was gritting his teeth when eventually he got his knee on to the higher sill, and then managed to kneel on it; there was little danger of falling.

The window was ajar.

He held his breath as he examined it, glad of the light of the moon, but then his heart sank. The fitting was exactly the same as that of his own room. He could get his hand inside, but he would not have sufficient freedom of movement to use his penknife on the screws.

He pulled at the window, but it would not open. He pushed it, but it did not move.

The night air was cold, and he shivered as a gust of wind went through him. He crouched there, unable to make up his mind. It was not far to the wall. He could get to the street and be in Whitehall within a few hours—he thought he was fairly near London, although he was not sure. In any case, he could reach a telephone kiosk and make a call to the office.

Then he nearly fell from the sill, for he heard a voice from within the room.

"Who is that?"

It was "Pamela." The moon shone on her pretty face and fair hair, and revealed her bare arms and her nightdress. She was close on the window, trying to see who it was; and she did not seem afraid.

Mike whispered: "It's Errol."

"The window won't open," she said, "it's no use. You must get away and bring help; there may never be such a chance again." Although her voice was pitched on a low key, he heard a new note in it; it held none of the vagueness of the first occasion when she had talked to him. As if reading his thought, she went on: "Don't take any notice of what I said the other day, that was only to hoodwink Brenn. *Please get away!* See my father—"

Her father, Brenn had said, had been killed in a raid on London. *Could* he depend on her?

"My father will help you," she said, "he lives in Chiswick. Peter Mandino—have you got that name? Peter Mandino."

"I've got it," said Mike. The shock of hearing the unusual name again nearly made him lose his balance. "All right—*are* you Pamela?"

"Yes. He knows who took me away; he'll believe you if you tell him the truth, but don't waste time! And don't let anyone but him know that I'm quite well again—do you understand?"

She broke off.

Errol had little warning, only a glow of light that came from the door of her room and gradually grew brighter. Then he saw a man outlined in the doorway. He thought it was Brenn. He slipped and nearly fell, but recovered himself by clinging to the drain-pipe. He saw the girl, who was clearly outlined against the light, turn and fling herself towards the newcomer, then he heard the muffled report of a shot. He turned and groped for the drain-pipe. He lost his grip with one hand, but managed to cling on and slide down. He dropped the last few feet and hit the ground with a thud which shook his whole body, but he had no time in which to think. He turned and made a bee-line for some trees fairly near the wall, jumped for a low bough, and swung himself up.

Light was shining from Pamela's room.

He saw a man's silhouette and expected a shot. None came, although soon he heard men's voices in the garden, and the opening and shutting of doors. He climbed as near the wall as he could, with the branch on which he was standing swaying wildly. It was several feet away from the wall, and he doubted whether it would give him purchase enough to jump and reach the wall. If he tugged at his shoulder too much, the harm would probably be done.

The voices grew nearer, and then Mike jumped.

Instinctively he used his uninjured arm to make the grip on the wall, and as it took his whole weight it was almost pulled out of its socket. He managed to hold on, supported himself with the other arm, and then dragged himself up until he was astride the wall. The trees sheltered him, and he swung his other leg over and dropped down. As he rose to his feet, he saw men coming out of the gateway of the house not very far away. He had no doubt that they were Brenn's men.

The shadow of the wall hid him from their sight, but when he moved he would have to go through a moonlit stretch, where he would be seen. The road was a wide one, and he could see the shapes of only two or three houses. His breathing grew easier. Two of the men went in the opposite direction and two came towards him.

Then he ran across the road.

"*There he is!*" The voice of one of the men came clearly through the silence, and there followed a soft, hissing sound like that of a silenced gun; he would be lucky if he escaped hurt. He heard the heavy thudding of their footsteps, but he reached the open gates of a house and turned in along the drive. There were trees and bushes, thick enough to give him cover; he plunged into them and, when he was well hidden, stopped again to regain his breath.

He could hear his pursuers calling to each other, but no one near. Refreshed, he tucked his elbows into his sides and raced round the house. There was no wall, only a hedge which separated the garden from a meadow, and he climbed the hedge. The voices of the men had faded, as if they had given up the search and were on their way back to the house.

Mike shivered in the cold. He could see the dark shapes of cows in the meadow and heard some of them moving. Turning back, he saw the house which he had just left, and several others, all built on a hill. Thanks to the moon he could see a town stretched out some distance away, dominated by the spire of a church; so he was on a hill. He turned and made his way towards the far end of the meadow, trying to make up his mind what best to do.

No one was about.

He squeezed through a hedge and looked along the road towards the house where he had been imprisoned. Everything was silent. He saw a post-box; just beyond it the name of the road was on a fence. He could just read that it was Hill Top Rise. Before long he reached a built-up area and found a telephone kiosk; the telephone had a St. Albans number.

"Hill Top Rise, St. Albans," Mike murmured, "and now all I want is some coppers. I—oh, what a fool!"

He slipped into the kiosk and dialled "O."

11

THE HOUSE AT HILL TOP RISE

The moon shone over the countryside, showing up the trees and hedges and the roofs of buildings, and shone over the town nestling in the valley. The men moved nearer Hill Top Rise, and two cars pulled up near one end and two near the other. From the first climbed Bill Loftus and Hammond. The shadowy figure of a local inspector approached them.

"Mr. Loftus?" he asked.

"That's right. Has there been any move?"

"No one's stirred," said the local man. "I think you've got them all right, sir."

"Good!" said Loftus, but he spoke more heartily than he felt, for he could not believe that Brenn and Witherspoon had made no attempt to get away. Acting on the assumption that they were still there, he exchanged a few words with Miller and the local police, and brought men nearer to the house. Then with Hammond and the youthful and eager Pip Evans, a dark-haired, amiable man who felt that he had failed signally in this case so far, and who was anxious to make amends, he approached the front of the house. The rear was closely guarded.

Loftus knocked on the door.

There was no response.

"We'll try a window," he said.

"Just the job for me," declared Pip, hopefully.

"All right," said Loftus. He knew that he would be clumsy if he tried to get through a window himself, so he waited in the porch while Evans and Hammond examined the nearest ground-floor window. It was not long before it was forced open, and it squeaked loudly. Pip Evans did not let that worry him. As soon as there was room he squeezed through. Hammond followed him, and the men in the grounds drew nearer.

Hammond shone a torch about the room, which was obviously a drawing-room. They went to the door, and Evans entered the passage where everything was very quiet.

"I don't like it much," said Hammond. "Open the front door, will you?"

Evans obeyed and Loftus stepped in. They stood together in the hall, looking about them, disappointed at the complete absence of sound. It seemed incredible that everyone had got away before the local police cordon had been put round the house.

"Call some of the others, Pip," he said.

Four Department men came in, hefty fellows who had heard what Loftus had said at the Renown Rooms and had seen Witherspoon; yet they could joke as they walked about the house, exploring first the ground floor and then the first, finding evidence that most of the rooms had been occupied, but no sign of any one present. There was a second floor and an attic; both were deserted.

"They move fast, don't they?" said Pip Evans *sotto voce*. "They don't seem to have left much behind, either."

"It's early to say that," said Loftus. "I wish I knew how they managed it." He stood frowning in the middle of the hall, then snapped his fingers and walked hurriedly into the kitchen, uttering the single word "cellar." They found the door to the cellar without much trouble, but it was locked, and they had to force it. There were no cobwebs, and the ceiling and the walls were distempered; the decoration looked comparatively recent. At the foot of the stairs was a small passage, leading to two doors, both of which were locked.

Loftus tapped against them, and said: "Steel, I fancy. That means we'll need an oxy-acetylene burner; we don't want to waste a lot of time trying without one. Pass the word back, will you?" he added, and word was carried up the stairs.

The workman who came with the burner asked no questions. Loftus asked him to tackle the nearer door first, and in fifteen minutes he had it open. When he swung it back it revealed a concrete passage and another steel door, which took him nearly as long to open.

Then they stepped into a long, narrow room, furnished as an office, but one corner was fitted with a bench, running water and the equipment of a small laboratory. A case filled with small drawers stood against one wall, and Loftus looked through it before he did anything else. Most of the drawers were empty, but a few held powders and some other odds and ends.

Loftus searched for a door which would lead out into the grounds. When he found it, it was not locked. It opened on to a passage which ran for nearly half a mile, rising gradually until they reached the exit, in a meadow beyond the grounds of the house. The police were nearer the house itself, and were taken by surprise when Loftus and his men appeared.

"So that's that," said Loftus, unable to keep the disappointment out of his voice. "They shut themselves in downstairs and had time to take away everything they wanted before we arrived. I suppose we ought to be satisfied at getting them out of one place." He sounded a long way from satisfied, however, and he peered about the meadow; torchlight revealed the clear marks of footprints which were traced to a side road, which had a sharp gradient. Near it was a large barn. In a few minutes they knew that the barn had been used as a garage, for it was redolent with the smell of oil and petrol. It was large enough for two cars, and Loftus had no doubt that they had been wheeled out of the garage and coasted downhill, so that they had not attracted the attention of the police.

"A complete wash-out," said Loftus, lighting a cigarette. "I wish—*what's that?*"

His voice dropped to a whisper, and his tone made the others with him swing round. He was looking through the open doors of the barn, and saw something white move on the other side of the road, a ghostly figure approaching them.

"That's Mike's *girl!*" snapped Loftus.

Hammond reached Pamela Mandino first.

She was dazed from a blow over the head, her nightdress was torn and her hair dishevelled. When they got her to the house they found that her feet were cut and bleeding and that her right side was badly bruised; but she was sensible and eager to talk.

Loftus, Hammond, Pip Evans and Superintendent Miller were with her in a downstairs room. She was sitting in an easy-chair, with a cup of tea in her hand and blankets wrapped about her. The electric fire was full on, and the room was uncomfortably warm for the men.

Pamela's face was flushed, and her blue eyes were very bright as she spoke of Mike.

"So he did get away," she said, and smiled breathlessly. "I didn't think he stood an earthly chance. I didn't dream he was the type of man who could get away with it!"

"Tell us just what happened after he had gone," said Loftus.

"Oh, just about what you might expect," said Pamela. "There was a lot of shouting, and Brenn gave the order to pack up and go. I think they had everything planned so that they could be out of the house in the shortest possible time. They took all the important papers out of the rooms and went downstairs with them—the place downstairs was once an air-raid shelter—and then they took me down."

"Mike said they had shot at you," Loftus told her.

"They really shot at him," she said. "Then they"—she bared her arm, showing the bruises—"hustled me downstairs, and I saw them packing everything up in the cellar. They made me walk along the passage, and gagged me when we reached the end. Then I was bundled into a car." She paused, looking bewildered. "Even now I don't know how I got away," she said. "They let me sit near the door. They were talking among themselves and the handle was quite near me. They had to slow down near the foot of the hill, and I opened the door and jumped out, but—"

Loftus said: "But what, Pamela?"

She seemed not to notice the use of her Christian name.

"It just wasn't like them," she said. "Usually they're so thorough, and if they'd given it a moment's thought they would have been able to stop me. I suppose they were too worked up about what had happened, and were careless. Anyhow, I didn't do myself much harm, because they were close to the edge of the road and I fell out on a grass bank. They didn't stop to come back for me. I walked back as soon as I felt I could move."

She was on edge with excitement, Loftus saw. He was eager to put more questions, and yet she looked too worn out to stand up to further questioning. "How long have you been here?"

He put the question more for the sake of it than anything else, but her answer made him start, and made Pip, Hammond and Miller stare at her incredulously.

"Three years," said Pamela Mandino. "*Three years!*"

Then she put her face in her hands and began to cry.

Mike Errol felt a new man.

Loftus had called for him before they had left St. Albans and he had driven back to town with Loftus, Hammond and Pamela, who had not fully recovered from her breakdown after telling them how long she had been imprisoned. Loftus had decided not to worry her with more questions immediately; in any case, he was anxious to get back to London.

Mike, sitting next to Pamela, glanced at her from time to time then smiled to himself. On the whole he did not think he had done such a bad job—a conclusion he had reached when he discovered that Loftus was emphatic that he had been undoubtedly right to get away. Mike had slept for four hours at the police station, and felt refreshed and exhilarated. He had told Loftus everything that he had heard and seen, including the fact that Pamela's father, the mysterious Mandino, lived in Chiswick. Loftus had made arrangement by telephone for the house to be located and for Mandino to be watched. His name was not in any directory, but the name of the previous tenant had been; that was why he had not been located before.

An odd thing was that Pamela had not mentioned her father to Loftus.

He went to his flat, where Christine, his wife, immediately took charge of Pamela and insisted that she should go to bed at once. She then made her more tea and gave her a sleeping tablet. Christine Loftus was a woman of understanding, possessed of good looks and a remarkable forbearance. She and Loftus had met in the course of one of the Department's affairs, and she knew a great deal about the working of the Department, although she never obtruded. Whatever Pamela might say would be reported as soon as Christine had the opportunity, and Loftus did not worry about her.

It was a little after seven o'clock.

He sat at the breakfast table with Mike and Hammond, and they tucked into bacon and eggs and drank copious draughts of tea. Loftus seemed much more good-tempered than he had been at St. Albans, and he related a little of what Mike did not know.

Mike scowled when he heard of Carruthers, and was silent for some time after he knew what had happened to Craigie, but his good spirits were not damped for long.

"It's just a matter of time," he said.

"Don't be too sanguine," said Hammond. He was in a brown study and had contributed little to the conversation. "One thing's certain, Bill—we want a talk with Mandino."

"Yes, it must be our first job," Loftus said. "I wonder if we ought to take Pamela back, or—"

"We'll size Mandino up first," said Hammond.

"Your word being law," murmured Loftus, but he raised no objections.

They drove to Tynham Place, Chiswick. It was a short, narrow road, a *cul-de-sac*, not far from the river, with three narrow houses on either side.

Loftus climbed out of the car as Mike rang the front-door bell. Further along Tynham Place, Pip Evans and another agent were in their car; they had followed Loftus just out of sight. Loftus was taking as few risks as possible.

A maid opened the door.

"Good morning," said Mike, "Is Mr. Mandino in?"

"I will inquire, sir," said the maid. "What name, please?"

"Errol," said Mike, "and—"

He did not finish, for as Loftus and Hammond were going up the stone steps to the front door a door in the hall opened and a man appeared. He made Mike start, for his hair was pure white and his face very pale; and both were emphasised by his black clothes. His well-marked eyebrows were as white as his hair, and he was clean shaven. He stared towards the door, and then said a curious thing.

"Where are they, Polly?"

"Just here, sir," said Polly, the maid, as Loftus and Hammond joined Errol in the hall. "A Mr. Errol, and two friends." She spoke quietly and did not look towards him.

"Errol—Errol—" repeated Mandino mildly. "I don't seem to recall the name."

"You won't know me, sir," said Mike Errol, advancing slowly.

He felt a sudden wave of misgiving and sympathy, combined. It was all too obvious that Mandino was blind. His fine eyes stared unseeingly towards the newcomers. His features were good, and there was a striking likeness between him and his daughter. His quiet voice was mellow and pleasing, and he smiled gravely.

"I am very busy," he said, "but if I can help you in any way, please tell me."

"That's good of you," said Mike. "This is Mr. Loftus, my chief, who is very anxious for a few words with you."

They followed Polly up the wide staircase to the first floor, into a long, narrow room, the windows of which overlooked the river and a stretch of grassland near Duke's Meadow, of boat-race fame. None of them spoke, but all were aware of the general sense of shock caused by the discovery of Mandino's blindness.

Loftus had expected a man with a touch of the sinister about him, someone not unlike Brenn or Witherspoon, and certainly not this gentle, mild-mannered old fellow. Like the others, he was trying to understand why Mike had once been asked by Brenn whether he worked for Mandino; Loftus was beginning to think that the question had been deliberately misleading.

Loftus said: "Mr. Mandino, your name was given to us by a man who calls himself Brenn."

"Brenn?" echoed Mandino. His expression did not alter, but there was a different tone in his voice. "In what connection did he suggest that you should come to see me, gentlemen?"

"He suggested that one of us was working for you," said Loftus, "and the circumstances were very curious, Mr. Mandino. I should have said before now that I am working on behalf of the police."

"Indeed?" said Mandino, dryly. "And Brenn passed my name on to the police, did he? Remarkable! Is he still working with Witherspoon?"

"Yes," said Loftus.

"I must tell you at once, gentlemen, that I have no love for either Brenn or Witherspoon. In fact, my infirmity, which you will have noticed, was entirely due to them. But you will not be interested in my troubles. How can I help you?"

Loftus said slowly:

"What can you tell us about either of them?"

"I can tell you that they are rogues, but you probably know that.

I can tell you that Brenn is a remarkable organiser and has a rather unusual brain, together with what might be called a lust for power. I can tell you, also, that Witherspoon, under the name of Rennett, was a brilliant doctor who specialised in eye treatment, but who was struck off for unprofessional conduct. I would be delighted to see them brought to justice, although it may be difficult to prove their many crimes."

"And yet, Mr. Mandino, you are not really being frank with us," said Loftus.

"I am at a loss to understand you," said Mandino, stiffly.

"I mean that you have not mentioned your daughter," said Loftus.

Mandino stood up, and rounded the desk, each movement quite swift and easy, as if he had done it a thousand times. He did not advance from the desk as he snapped:

"What do you know of my daughter?"

"That Brenn and Witherspoon hold her," said Loftus.

"Brenn would not have told you that!"

"We found out without his help," said Loftus.

Mandino drew in his breath and advanced, his hands stretched out in front of him and his eyes very wide open. It was hard to realise that he could not see.

"Where is she? If you can release her then I can perhaps help you more, but while she is in their hands, mine are tied."

"Before we can act we must know more about Brenn."

"I do not understand you! If you can find my daughter, then it is your duty to make her free!"

"There are bigger things at stake than individuals," Loftus said, and Mike, watching the old man's face, admired Loftus' approach and knew that he himself would never have thought of acting like this. The bait to entice Mandino to tell the full story was the freedom of Pamela; if the old man knew that she was already free he might not talk. "Mr. Mandino, every effort will be made to see that your daughter comes to no harm," Loftus continued, "but before we raid the house where she is a prisoner we must make sure that no great risks are taken in other matters. Other people and other things are at stake."

At last Mandino said:

"What do you expect me to tell you? I would never have believed that officers of the law would have adopted such a method, one worthy of Brenn himself."

"In the past few months a number of important people have been made blind by Witherspoon," said Loftus quietly. "Others are threatened. He might harm the country, as well as individuals, so the stakes are very high. Pamela is comparatively unimportant, but every effort will be made to help her once we dare act."

"Once you *dare*," said Mandino, wonderingly. "So Brenn has such power as that? I am beginning to understand," he went on. "He always said that he would perform miracles, and I think we can say that he has done so. You understand that I have not seen him for a long time—over two years—and I am not up to date with his ambitions and his plans."

"Tell us what you can," said Loftus.

"I will. He is the dictatorial type. When he first began to exert his influence he sought money and industrial power. I think he still does."

"Go on," said Loftus; the others exchanged glances.

"Gradually, over a long period, he bought up interests in industrial concerns. In fact, Brenn, Witherspoon and myself were partners, and I still retain some of the interests. He has a corner—I think that is the expression—in certain basic industries. Steel, shipping, plastics and alloys—and his interests are very strong indeed. I doubt whether it is known that he is such a powerful influence behind the scenes, but you would be surprised to know how deep his influence is."

"I see," said Loftus, and he looked much more satisfied.

"That is practically all I can tell you. There was a time when I had a list of the companies and corporations in which he held an interest, but he took that away when I was first stricken with blindness. I remember some of them—I have a list in my desk. You would like it, of course?"

"I would," said Loftus.

Mandino went to his desk, drew out a file and opened it, then picked up a single typewritten sheet of paper.

"This is it, Mr. Loftus."

"Thank you," said Loftus.

He felt tense with excitement as he ran his eye down the list. He saw twenty or more names mentioned, covering most industries. They were in alphabetical order, but there was no indication of the strength of Brenn's holding.

Mandino spoke quietly.

"I have tried not to exaggerate, but I should tell you that Brenn is not only a remarkable man but a very careful and thorough one. He has ability as well as extravagant ideas. If his mind were not perverted—there is no other explanation of his behaviour—he would exert a very beneficial influence, for his brain is one which we could use to great advantage in this country. Do not be persuaded to under-estimate him, Mr. Loftus."

"I won't," said Loftus. "I—"

He stopped abruptly.

From the street there came the hoot of a car horn—three quick blasts. It was a signal from Pip Evans and his companion that there was need for caution. The window did not overlook the street, and Loftus turned abruptly towards the door.

"What is the matter?" demanded Mandino sharply.

"I don't know," said Loftus.

He did not go out, for Mike Errol moved swiftly towards the door and reached the landing, which had a window overlooking the street corner where Pip had been. He could not see Pip or the other man, or the car. There were three or four men walking down the street towards the house, but before he turned back to tell Loftus he heard a familiar voice from the foot of the stairs.

"Don't try to climb out of *another* window," said Brenn, and Mike stared down at the man as he mounted the stairs, with an automatic in his hand.

By Mike's side was a tall earthenware vase, filled with chrysanthemums. Brenn was half-way up the stairs, and behind him were several other men: Mike recognised Henry and the red-faced "undertaker," Jackman. Brenn was smiling, composed and quite sure of himself.

Mike kicked the vase down the stairs. Water poured out of it, drenching Brenn, who tried to dodge to one side but could not get out of the way in time. The vase struck his legs and broke. Water cascaded down the stairs, but Henry leapt over the broken pieces, his vicious expression far more threatening than Brenn's.

He fired at once.

He missed, for Mike, knowing that the odds were hopeless, had swung round towards the room from which Hammond was coming, with Loftus just behind him.

"Too strong a party," Mike snapped. "The window!"

Another shot hit the wall near him. He pushed Hammond inside the room and nearly knocked Loftus over. Three of Brenn's men were at the head of the stairs, and Hammond slammed and locked the door as Mike reached the window. Hammond pushed a chair beneath the door-handle for greater security. The glass smashed as a bullet struck it and buried itself in the ceiling. Mike caught a glimpse of a man at the window of the house across the street before another shot was fired and he moved swiftly out of range, standing behind the wall.

Loftus and Hammond were on the other side of the window and Mandino was by his desk, standing quite still. He was looking towards the door.

"An assault force," Mike said lightly. "I'm afraid we're going to have big trouble, Bill."

"Why be pessimistic?" asked Loftus, with a grin.

"That foolish conversation may buoy your spirits up," said Brenn from the other side of the door, "but it will do you no good at all. Open the door, Loftus, I have to talk to you."

"The door needn't stop us from talking," said Loftus.

"I shall not forgive you if you are obstinate," said Brenn. He seemed to be breathing heavily. "Don't imagine that you can get away. Don't think you can use the telephone—it has been put out of order, but is *not* registering as such on the exchange. There are six houses in the *cul-de-sac*, and I own them all. They are occupied by my workers. Mandino was foolish enough to think that I would let him live here without being under supervision, but I knew that sooner or later you would find him. Every possible precaution has been taken, and all the weapons are silent ones. You are too far away from anywhere for your shouts to attract attention, and—"

"You should hear me shout," said Loftus, and went straight into a terrific bellow which must have been heard a quarter of a mile away.

"*Police!*" he roared. "*Police!* Ahoy, there—*police!*"

"Be quiet!" snapped Brenn.

"This is only a beginning," said Loftus, "when we all shout together you'll hear something! Come on, now, one, two, three—*police!*"

On the last word Hammond and Mike joined in and the room echoed to the shout, the echoes went up and down Tynham Place and across the river and to the streets near by; they must inevitably have attracted attention.

"All right," said Brenn.

The words sounded ridiculously weak, but there was more behind them than Loftus liked. Brenn gave soft-voiced instructions to the men with him. Loftus could not catch all the words, but thought that plans had been made to meet this eventuality. He was prepared for anything, from an attempt to gas them out to a spattering of machine-gun bullets on the door or an attempt to break it down; but for some minutes all he heard was the footsteps of men running up and down the stairs.

Mike edged towards the window.

A bullet struck it not two inches from his head, and he dodged back again quickly; it was all the proof he needed that the place was surrounded. Mandino still stood staring towards the window, without expression. Hammond had his automatic in his hand, but there was nothing any of them could do.

Brenn called: "I will give you one more chance to open the door, Loftus. Don't reject it."

"Altogether, now," said Loftus, "one, two, three—*police!* Now the name of the place. One, two, three—*Tynham Place!*" As the echoes faded he spoke in a more normal voice. "I shouldn't stay too long, Brenn."

The answer was a sudden streak of flame which came beneath the door. It was either burning petrol or liquid fire; liquid fire was the more likely, for it ran a couple of yards into the room and the carpet burned almost as soon as it was touched. It reached a chair, which was soon enveloped in flames. Smoke poured from the fire, and more fire came from under the door, running in little rivulets in all directions.

Mandino snapped: "There is smoke!"

"It's worse than that," said Loftus, "come on, Mike!" He pushed Mandino aside and reached the desk. Hammond and Mike joined him, and between them they lifted the desk and carried it towards the door. They turned it upside down, drawers and papers falling out and being devoured by the fire, but they put it on its back across the doorway and over the flames. Only a little stretch of carpet remained on fire, but Errol beat that out with a steel filing tray, and Loftus picked up the burning chair and flung it out of the window. The heavy oak of the desk would not resist the flames for long, but it would give them at least ten minutes' respite.

"Are you all right, Mr. Mandino?" said Loftus, brushing his hair from his eyes and incidentally smearing his forehead with smuts.

Mandino said nothing.

"I ought to tell you now that Pamela is quite safe," said Loftus, "and you needn't worry about her."

Mandino cried: "She is!"

"Loftus, if you don't come out—" began Brenn.

"Oh, go away!" snapped Loftus, testily, "we haven't time to talk to you." He drew a deep breath and choked, for the room was filled with smoke and getting unbearably hot, while they could hardly see the far wall. "We ought to be all right near the window," he added, more quietly.

"That corner over there is freer than anywhere else," said Hammond. "Mr. Mandino—" he took the old man's arm and led him to the corner which, by some trick of the draught, was fairly clear. They stood huddled together, while the fire increased and the smoke got thicker; breathing grew difficult. Obviously the fire was in the passage as well as in the room. They could hear nothing but the crackling of the flames, and had no idea of what was happening in the street, for their view was blocked with a pall of smoke.

Hammond spoke at last.

"I'll see what's happening outside."

"I'm coming," said Mike.

"You'd better stay. You've had quite enough bother with your arm already." Hammond reached the window, confident that he could not be seen, and climbed out.

It was a tall house, and the drop to the paved area below was a long one. His eyes were watering, and even if the smoke had not been there it would have been difficult for him to see about him. He let himself down at full stretch, his feet moving to and fro as he tried to find a porch, or else something to which he could cling.

He could see no one in the street.

His arms began to ache, and his fingers were very hot. He looked upwards, and saw through the smoke that there was a ledge above the window and another just above that; he would do better to try to get to the roof. He tried to haul himself up, but as he did so he heard the roar of an engine from not far away. He waited, still hanging at arm's length. Then a gust of wind blew the smoke away, and he caught a glimpse of a fire-fighting unit, with three firemen already running towards the house. He heard voices, and he raised his own.

"*Get—a—ladder!*"

He felt sure then that they would get out in time; his only anxiety was whether Brenn would have enough men at hand to try to prevent the firemen from doing their work of rescue. After a few minutes a long ladder was run up, and a fireman mounted it without hindrance. Hammond was able to climb down, although he was choking with the smoke and his head was reeling. Another fireman went up immediately after him. Mandino was carried to safety, and then Loftus began to feel his way down the ladder, missing several times with his artificial leg but eventually reaching the ground. He was followed by Mike, who came down with remarkable agility.

The ceiling of the room fell in as the first jet of water began to play near the window.

Mandino was still conscious, but he seemed struck dumb. Mike kept a hand on his arm and led him towards the end of the *cul-de-sac*, where a crowd of people had already gathered. Policemen were hurrying towards the spot, and there was no sign of Brenn or Henry, although Mike knew that some in the crowd might be Brenn's men. He saw Pip Evans and the other Department man being carried by two ambulance men. There was no sign of the maid.

"Bruce, there's Pip," said Mike quietly.

Hammond looked towards the men. They were unconscious and so limp that they might be dead. Hammond hurried over to them and Mike watched tensely until Hammond turned round and cocked a thumb. Loftus, who was surveying the firemen at work, just caught sight of the gesture.

"We can't complain," he said. "I—my oath, look at that!"

At the end house of the three on the same side as Mandino's a plume of smoke curled from the top-floor window. Hardly had Loftus drawn attention to it than another and another came, followed by flames. The firemen, startled at such an outbreak and momentarily nonplussed, sent for another unit; but before it arrived the houses on the other side were alight; those fires were not started by sparks from the first outbreak.

Loftus drew a deep breath.

"He's thorough," he said, "and he's burning the lot down. But we *are* making progress."

Mike said: "Backwards or forwards?" He coughed, and his grip on Mandino's arm tightened. The older man was clearly still too shocked to give any thought to the missing maid.

"*Look out!*" cried Loftus, in sudden alarm.

The move took him so much by surprise that it nearly came off. He was looking towards the end of the *cul-de-sac*. The crowd was being pressed back by the police, but straining forward in spite of the danger. He did not see who threw the thing, but he did see what looked like a hand-grenade flying through the air. Mike also saw it. He tugged at Mandino's arm and flung himself forward. Loftus went down with several of the men who had been alarmed by his cry. Hammond was on his feet when the hand-grenade hit the ground and exploded, and the blast was enough to bowl him over. He was not hurt, although pieces of metal flew in all directions, and were lost in the smoke and flames. Two firemen were hit and had to be given first aid.

Mandino was not touched.

"For a few hours Mandino's the most precious thing we've got," said Loftus, grimly, "because he knows some of the companies Brenn is interested in. Keep him safe, Mike. We mustn't take chances, because Brenn knows the risk, too."

He moved off, limping, to find the nearest telephone, while Hammond and Mike stood on either side of Mandino, who had not uttered a word.

12

"QUITE A JOURNEY"

"Well, well," said Loftus, grinning broadly, "I call that quite a journey!"

Blackened and dishevelled, with his clothes singed and torn, he sat back in an easy-chair at his flat and regarded his wife. She had been so taken aback by his appearance that she forgot to protest at his sitting down without putting a cover on the chair.

Mike and Hammond were in the front room of the flat with them, and Mandino was in the bedroom. He had not spoken from the moment he had been put into a car near the burned houses. At the back and front of the flat armed police were on guard, for it was a time to take every possible precaution. Miller had gladly co-operated.

"And you look quite a mess," said Christine, but there was relief in her fine eyes.

"How's Pamela?" asked Loftus. "I mean, how has she been?"

"Sleeping, most of the time," said Christine, "but she's probably awake now—shall I call her?"

"I'll go," said Loftus.

He hoisted himself to his feet and went across to the spare room, opening the door quietly. Pamela was still in bed and asleep. One arm, covered in a sleeve of Christine's pyjamas, was over the bed-spread. Her lips were closed, and for the first time he saw how really lovely she was. He watched her even breathing for a few seconds, and then closed the door.

He believed that Mandino would recover more quickly if he were left on his own, and they had lunch before he washed the worst of the dirt and smuts off his face and went into the bedroom. He doubted whether Mandino had realised the dangers of the journey; now, as the pale, smoke-grimed face turned towards him, he thought that he had never seen such sadness in a man's eyes.

"This is Loftus," he said.

"I thought so," said Mandino.

"How are you feeling?"

"I hardly know," said Mandino, "I hardly know. Everything gone—everything. Even my books." He drew in his breath, and then frowned. A curious transformation came over him as he stared towards Loftus, and when he spoke again it was in a sharper voice. "Loftus! *What* did you say about my daughter? *What did you say?*"

Loftus said: "She is quite safe, and in this flat."

"Here?" said Mandino incredulously. "You—you *meant* what you said? Pamela is—*here!*"

"She's sleeping," Loftus said, "but she'll be in with you before long. Both of you are quite safe now, you know. Brenn will be able to do you no harm."

There was a feeling of anti-climax later in the afternoon.

The reunion of Pamela and her father, skilfully managed by Christine and observed by no one at the flat, was the high-light. Loftus could not get in touch with Hershall, although he went to see Craigie and passed on all the information. He telephoned the Chiswick Fire Station, to be told that the fires were under control, but that so far there had been no trace of human remains in Tynham Place. It would be some hours before a final report could be made, however; the fate of Polly, the maid-and-general factotum, remained obscure. There was no sign of Brenn and no indication of where he had gone to earth.

Loftus felt lost without Craigie. He did not feel that he could do anything on the strength of the list which Mandino had given him until he had consulted Hershall. Another problem presented itself: what to do with Mandino and Pamela; he could not keep them at the flat indefinitely, and they must be somewhere under guard. He wanted to cross-examine them, but the right moment had not yet come.

Mike and Hammond had gone to Woking to see Carruthers and Hartley. Except that the professor had recovered his sight there was little that they knew of recent events at Lyddon House, and Loftus was anxious for a full report as soon as he could get it. Forbeson had instructions to get a sample of the lotions which Witherspoon had sent for the treatment, of course, and Loftus, sitting in his flat and working up a report for Hershall, did not seriously doubt that the sample would be obtained.

Carruthers appeared to have resigned himself to his blindness. After his one outburst against Witherspoon he had made no protest, and, being so fit physically, he did not need to keep to his bed. He felt his way about the Guest House, and his voice was cheerful when he heard Martha; he might not have been so cheerful had he been able to see the tears in her eyes when she came upon him unexpectedly, groping his way from room to room.

Jim Dale had little to say.

Witherspoon had left the Guest House on the day of the meeting at the Renown Rooms and had not returned. His luggage was still there, and every case and trunk had been searched without yielding any evidence. The Guest House was watched by several of the Department men, who took turns with those who were keeping an eye on Lyddon House. Nothing had happened to attract their attention and they were all feeling bored with life.

Hammond and Mike went on to Lyddon House.

Julia saw them from a window, and had the door open by the time they reached it. She looked younger and less careworn.

"Well, how are things?" asked Hammond.

"Splendid!" said Julia. "I—why, *Mike!*"

"Back again and sound in wind and limb," said Mike grinning, "and you can ignore the superficial scratches, my poppet. Congratulations and all that."

"It's *wonderful!*" declared Julia. "I've been spending the whole morning persuading Daddy that now he's over it he must get away for a few weeks and have a complete rest. You'll add your pleas, won't you? *Nothing* can be so important that he can't have a rest."

"I think it's a good idea," said Hammond. "I'd like to have a few words with him, and I'll say so. May I go up?"

"Of course," said Julia. "What about you, Mike?"

"I'll leave it to the big chief," said Mike, and Hammond went upstairs, while the couple stayed in the drawing-room.

"The only thing that has worried me a little," said Julia, "is that the man Mrs. McFarlane managed to get hold of disappeared this morning."

"Oh," said Mike, controlling a start. "What kind of man?"

"Ass! He was very good about the house; things wouldn't have gone half as well if it hadn't been for him. He was here first thing, and then he went to the village—at least, he said he was going. He wasn't seen by anyone, and he hasn't come back. I suppose he's taken French leave for the day," she went on, and branched off into something else.

Hammond came downstairs soon afterwards.

For obvious reasons, Julia had not been told that the missing Forbeson was a member of the Department, and as soon as they were in the car and Julia had gone indoors, Mike said urgently:

"Bruce, there's more bother; Forbeson is missing."

Hammond was letting in the clutch; he crashed it badly.

"Is he, by George! He's getting that lotion. How long has he been gone?"

"Since about ten o'clock," said Mike. "Our fellows were round and about, weren't they?"

"Of course." Hammond started off and drove to the end of the drive, but he stopped just round the corner and called a man who was lurking in a copse—a tall, weary-looking fellow, with a long, drooping moustache.

"Have you seen Forbeson?" Hammond asked sharply.

"No," said the other, "he hasn't been about."

"He left the house about ten and didn't get back," said Hammond. "See what you can find out, will you?"

The man with the drooping moustache looked troubled, promised that he would do everything he could, and hurried off. Hammond started the car again, but before he spoke they came within sight of the Guest House, and outside it was the unmistakable green monstrosity which Loftus called a car. The vintage Bentley would not have looked so bad had it not been painted recently, and had the paint not been so vivid.

"Now what's he up to?" said Mike.

Hammond said nothing. He pulled up in front of the Guest House and they went in. Loftus' voice could be heard coming from the kitchen, alternating with Martha's and with an occasional word from Jim Dale. Loftus, it seemed, was asking them if they felt really sure about some mysterious matter, and they were reassuring him.

He was leaning against the kitchen sink, and Martha was sitting on the kitchen table, with her neat legs crossed and her innocent eyes wide open. Dale was sitting on the only chair, smoking a pipe. It was a pleasant little domestic scene.

"Now what?" asked Hammond, going inside.

"Why, hallo!" said Loftus. "I had an idea, old man, and thought I'd better discuss it with the Dales in person. It's about the Mandinos. Now that Witherspoon has gone they've just got room for Pamela and the old chap. They're willing to take the risks that might turn up, so it's settled."

"Good," said Hammond, perfunctorily.

Loftus eyed him curiously.

"Don't you agree that it's wise?"

"I don't see anything against it," said Hammond. "The position is all right, and if the Dales don't mind taking a chance it's as good a place as any, since we've got to have the district well covered. Bill, Forbeson's disappeared from the house. You know what that means, don't you?"

Loftus stiffened.

"How long has he been gone?"

"Several hours. I've started the others looking for him, but I doubt now whether they will get what really matters."

"What does *really* matter?" asked Martha, eagerly.

"The samples of the lotions which cured Hartley," said Loftus. "Forbeson doubtless managed to get hold of them, and the probability is that he was watched and the stuff stolen from him. What happened to him is anyone's guess, but the most curious point about the whole business is this: how did whoever attacked him get past our fellows?"

"They aren't infallible," said Mike, slowly.

"They would have stopped anything within reason," Loftus said. "It's a queer business, and I don't like it. It needn't upset our arrangements," he went on, looking at Martha, who shook her head emphatically and said something about it being very thrilling.

An hour later, when the news was received that Forbeson had been found dead in a shrubbery about two hundred yards from Lyddon House itself, she did not call it thrilling—but she gave no sign that she regretted what she and her husband had agreed to do.

"I don't see that you can blame yourself," Hershall said. "You tried not to make it obvious that you knew what was happening; that was the right policy."

"I have doubts," said Loftus. "Witherspoon must have realised that he would be after the lotion, and could not see how we could get it. By giving him no false trail, we made him look in unlikely places. When he did that, Forbeson stood out a mile. The method was too tortuous, sir. I would have staked my life on getting something for Faversham to play with."

"Don't harass yourself with regrets," Hershall said, sharply. "You've more than enough to do, and you haven't been without results entirely, you know. You seem to have forced Brenn on to the defensive for a little while, and there have been no new instances of blindness."

"We don't know what's brewing," said Loftus, tugging at his pipe. "It might take several weeks for the stuff to work—Craigie may have been dosed some time before, so might Carruthers. We know so little about it that—" he broke off and grinned. "I'm sorry, sir! This show has got under my skin from the very beginning. There's something about it which I can't fathom. I can't see through it to the possibilities. For instance, Brenn threw Mandino at our heads, and from Mandino we've learned all that we know about Brenn. Why did he make the mistake?"

"Did he know that Errol worked with you?" asked Hershall pertinently.

"No," said Loftus. "I'd missed that—just another temporary blind spot, I'm afraid."

"What are you doing with this man Mandino?" Hershall asked.

"We've taken him to the Guest House at Woking. I've questioned him and got a story which I think is the true one. He and Brenn fell out because Brenn was taking risks and breaking the law in several directions. Brenn blinded him and, when Mandino still kept trying to work against him, kidnapped his daughter. There are a lot of details to be filled in, but they are the main points."

"The most worrying feature is the fact that it has been going on for so many years," said Hershall. "Is this Guest House safe enough?"

"It's as safe as anywhere," said Loftus. "Carruthers will stay, as well as the Dales, to make it look normal. It's well placed, with half an acre of ground surrounded by a thick hedge, every corner of which can be watched. It's handy for Lyddon Hall, and there may be a chance of playing Hartley and Mandino off against each other."

"Hartley?" Hershall was startled.

"I don't think we can take him or anyone else for granted," said Loftus. "This business goes too deep." He stared at the Prime Minister, and his expression grew preoccupied.

"There's something floating about my mind like a word on the tip of my tongue," he said. "I can't quite get it, but when I do it might give us the answer. I take it that you want me to carry on as I am doing?"

"Yes," said Hershall. "What about these companies which Mandino mentioned?"

"I kept the list, sir, and it's with Miller at the Yard. A careful investigation into the companies and the shareholders is being made, and when Miller learns anything which may be helpful, he'll get in touch with me."

"So you'll let me know," said Hershall. "Right, Loftus! Now, I must be off."

He went out, and as he passed through the sliding door Loftus watched him and wondered what would happen if he or other key men in the Government were suddenly stricken with blindness. He had wondered before, and the thought had affected him with a sense of horror and impotency which partly explained his uncertain nerves and outbursts of irritation. Any satisfaction he had felt at getting Mandino away faded; it no longer seemed important. The fact remained, however, that Brenn had gone to extreme length to try to kill Mandino.

Was that to try to prevent Mandino from talking about the past— or was Mandino still holding something back?

Loftus decided that a longer talk with the blind man and his daughter was the next thing on the list, but before he left the office to go to his flat a green light showed in the mantelpiece. He pressed the button, and, when the door slid open, Mike Errol slipped through.

"Howdy!" he said, raising a hand. "Still thinking?"

"Still trying to," said Loftus, shortly.

"Curious thing, but so have I," said Mike, owlishly. "I don't know whether I've told you, or whether Carruthers realised it, or whether Julia Hartley came across—I do know that I meant to make more of it before."

"Of what?" asked Loftus.

"Fergus Grey—remember him?" asked Mike. "He was one of the johnnies who interested us once upon a time, but I gather he's faded out just lately. Right?"

"Partly right. He's still being watched. We know the curious family position and that there's no love lost between him and his uncle, and we know that Brenn has something on him," said Loftus.

"He pretended to be drunk," said Mike. "Operative word, pretended."

"Pretended, yes," echoed Loftus.

"So it sinks in," said Mike. "Yes—he rolled up to Hartley's house on the night when things went wrong, and he acted drunk. He wasn't. He cleared off without giving us any idea why he came, but he must have had a reason."

Loftus spoke thoughtfully.

"This show is really getting beyond me—yes, you reported it to Gordon by telephone, but it completely slipped my mind. We want to know why he pretended to be drunk; it's more important than anything else as far as his part is concerned."

"So what do I do?" asked Mike.

"Go down to Woking and get him along to the Guest House some time this evening," said Loftus. "I'll be there—or if I can't make it, Bruce will be. Okay?"

"Yessir!" said Mike, and grinned and went out.

Loftus hoped for more information from Pamela, but her story was straightforward and simple. It was three years since she had been prevented from returning to her home, and she had been at the St. Albans house all the time. She had been subjected to rigorous cross-examination after she had been there a few weeks, because Brenn wanted to know her father's plans. As a result, she admitted frankly, she had been ill; she now knew that she had suffered from delusions.

She had realised that after about eighteen months, when she was returning to normal. She had overcome the temptation to reveal the fact that she was on the mend, for if she remained "simple" she was in less danger. Brenn and Witherspoon had let her live fairly freely and had been tolerant with her. Brenn had invented the story of her parents being dead and her husband killed; he had also invented her "child to be."

"There were times when I thought he and Witherspoon were trying to find out just how much I would believe about myself," said Pamela. "I know it all sounds extremely unlikely, but—I *was* there for three years!"

"Yes," said Loftus. "And in that time you made no serious attempt to find her, Mr. Mandino?"

"I made a great number of attempts," said Mandino, "but I never succeeded. I employed detectives of repute; I even got in touch with one or two whom I knew were not particularly law-abiding, but the result was always the same. There was no trace. Brenn had told me that if I gave any information against him to the police, Pamela would be smitten with blindness. Can you understand that at all costs I felt that I had to preserve her sight?"

Loftus looked at him thoughtfully.

"I suppose I can," he said, "but—isn't there something else? Oh, should I say, wasn't there? Could Brenn have lodged information with the police that would have earned you a long term of imprisonment, for instance?" He spoke mildly, looking at Pamela and not the old man. Her face was blank.

"I was affected by no consideration other than my daughter's welfare," Mandino said. "My affairs have always been above board and open for inspection, Mr. Loftus. I wish I could make you understand what it feels like to be in my position."

"I think I can," said Loftus, after a pause. "All right—we'll take that as read! Now, Pamela—"

He plied her with questions, but her sojourn at St. Albans had been amazingly quiet. She knew something of what had been going on, and knew that Witherspoon had been carrying out researches for a cure, as well as a cause, for blindness, but she had been too closely watched to learn a great deal. She had seen a chance of getting news outside when she had first met Errol, which explained her attitude with him.

That was all.

Loftus, not altogether convinced, decided to accept it for the time being, and early in the evening he drove them down to Woking. They sat at the back of the car, and there were two cars with them—one ahead and one behind—as well as two motor-cyclists, who were never far away. Christine sat in the front with Loftus.

The journey was accomplished without incident. But as they drew near the Guest House Loftus heard an exclamation from Pamela, and when he turned he saw that she was staring along the road towards Mike Errol—who was walking towards them with Fergus Grey. The evening sun was shining on Grey's hair, making it look very bright. He was walking leisurely, and Mike appeared to be getting on famously with him; certainly there was no evidence of strain between them.

Loftus looked at Pamela.

She was standing up in the open car staring towards the couple—and it could not have been Mike who startled her. Grey had not yet noticed her.

"Pamela, my dear," said Mandino, "what is worrying you?"

"It—it doesn't matter," she said. "I—I thought I saw someone I knew." She sat down hastily and averted her face, but Fergus Grey had seen her.

He stopped still, staring.

Mike turned to him, puzzled.

"What were you saying?"

"Er—nothing, nothing," said Grey, and before Mike realised what he was about to do he turned and began to hurry away from the Guest House. Everyone watching him saw the pallor of his face.

13

THE CURIOUS BEHAVIOUR OF
FERGUS GREY

Mike turned in Grey's wake.

Loftus got out of the car slowly, and Christine helped first Pamela and then her father to get out. The girl was staring after Grey and Mike, both of whom were nearly out of sight.

Men were stationed about the house; one of them was the man with the drooping moustache. His name was Pitt, and he was feeling his failure to save Forbeson very keenly. Loftus signalled to him, and Pitt began to hurry in Mike's wake. Mike, glancing over his shoulder, saw that with satisfaction.

Grey reached the gates of Lyddon House.

He did not seem to realise that he was being followed—or, if he did, he did not care. He swung along the drive, half-walking, half-running, and Mike had to lengthen his stride to keep close to him. He reached the porch fifty feet ahead of Mike and thundered on the door.

Mike saw Mrs. McFarlane open the door, her expression forbidding, but Grey pushed past her without a word. She looked as if she would try to stop him, but instead she stared after him. Mike reached the porch.

"Good afternoon," he said, politely.

"Who—" began Mrs. McFarlane, and then she found herself staring at Mike's back as he also went up the stairs.

Grey reached Hartley's study.

The door was closed, but the tapping of a typewriter was audible. It grew louder as Grey opened the door and strode in, then it stopped abruptly. Mike drew nearer. Grey made no attempt to close the door, but stood staring at Hartley, who was rising slowly to his feet.

The lined face of the economist, who had aged considerably in the short period of his blindness, grew set. He was nearly white-haired, and Mike had a shock when he saw him; but before he had time to think, Hartley said:

"I have forbidden you this house. Get out!"

Grey's voice was harsh with strain.

"Do you know who is in Woking? Pamela Mandino, and I think Mandino himself. Lord knows you've done little to deserve help from me, but with Mandino in the neighbourhood your life won't be worth a tinker's cuss!"

"You have come here talking the most arrant nonsense," said Hartley, coldly.

"All right—you've asked for it," said Grey, savagely.

He swung round, and for the first time he became aware of Mike's presence. He started, and some colour returned to his cheeks. Then his lips tightened and he pushed past Mike, who decided that the time was ripe to talk to Hartley and to allow Pitt to follow Fergus Grey.

So he smiled and said: "Why, hallo!"

"Good evening, Mr. Errol," Hartley said frigidly.

"I've got to congratulate you, and all that, on the recovery of the peepers," said Mike brightly. "I mean, quite a relief, wasn't it? Er—Fergus seems worried."

"Fergus Grey is a young lout in whom I have no interest whatsoever," said Hartley. "Mr. Errol, I appreciate the interest that you and your friends have taken in me, and I am aware that you may have had something to do with my recovery, but I resent your coming into this house without the courtesy of asking permission—and I am extremely busy."

"Oh," said Mike.

Throughout the exchanges Julia had sat at the desk with a pencil in her hand and the typewriter in front of her. Now she looked at Mike. Her expression was partly one of puzzlement, but she seemed to be asking Mike to make allowances for her father's attitude. It was a strange set-up, and Mike began to wish that he were not on his own.

His wish was granted quickly.

They heard a ring, and the front door was opened so quickly that obviously Mrs. McFarlane had been near. Loftus' voice followed.

"Good afternoon," he said, politely, did not pause for reply, and hurried up the stairs.

Hartley stood up and snapped: "I refuse to allow myself to be interrupted any further!"

Loftus came in, nodded and smiled, and then sat heavily on an upright chair. His composure seemed to baffle Hartley. Julia frowned, and the point of her pencil snapped.

"What's been doing, Mike?" Loftus asked.

"I see no reason—" began Hartley.

"I was not speaking to you, sir," said Loftus, and his voice boomed out. His manner reduced Hartley to silence as he looked at Mike again. "Well?" His expression was forbidding.

Mike said: "Grey reported the appearance of the Mandinos to Hartley. Hartley says that he knows nothing of them. Grey went out breathing threats. *Finis.*" He entered into the spirit of Loftus' attitude, and he made Julia get to her feet, her brow darkening.

"This is impertinence!" snapped Hartley.

"Listen to me," said Loftus, softly. "You have played a curious part in this affair, Sir Basil, and we have reached the stage when we want everything explained—past, present and future. The time for the velvet gloves is past, because the issues are too large. What do you know of Mandino?"

"Nothing!"

Loftus said: "I don't believe you."

Hartley flared up. "I will not be insulted."

"Unless you answer, you will be taken to London for interrogation," said Loftus, and went on quickly: "Yes, I have the necessary authority."

Hartley did not speak. He gave no impression of being alarmed, and for the first time Loftus wondered if his own attitude was justified. He had decided, however, that the time for going cautiously had passed.

It was Julia who broke the ensuing silence.

"You can't be serious, Mr. Loftus! My father is leaving here to-morrow, and—"

"I am quite serious," said Loftus, abruptly.

"Perhaps you will be good enough to tell me by what extraordinary reasoning you have reached this conclusion," said Hartley, angrily.

"That's easy," said Loftus. "At first it looked all odds that you were a victim, but you're the only victim that has recovered. There must be a reason for that."

"This man had endeavoured to show you that he can cure the condition!"

"But why pick on you—why not on someone who has less specialised knowledge?" asked Loftus. "On the other hand, if you and he were working together, and you refused to do something he wanted, he might blind you to frighten you and also to confuse us. Then, when you came to heel—ah! That stung, didn't it?"

"Nonsense!" snapped Hartley, but he was going pale.

"I don't think so," said Loftus, "and I'm not going to take any risks. There is another pointer: Mandino was once a colleague of Brenn's, and you were warned of his impending arrival. You were afraid—"

"You *might* be right," said a voice from the door.

Both Mike and Loftus swung round and found themselves looking into the face of Mrs. McFarlane, as well as into the muzzle of an automatic which she held steadily in front of her. It covered both men.

On Julia's face there was an expression of sheer amazement; Mike saw that out of the corner of his eye. Hartley obviously had been expecting it, for he stood up and there was a half-smile on his lips.

"If they move, shoot to kill," he said. "You've done very well, Jeanie. I was hoping you wouldn't wait much longer." He stood up and pushed his chair back. "Julia, you must not interest yourself in this. It is nothing to do with you, and if you interfere you might get hurt. I shall be going away for a while, and I may not come back at all. If I don't I will send for you when everything is safe." He took a cigarette from a box on the desk, lit it, and looked into Loftus' face. "When did you first begin to suspect me, Loftus?"

"Soon enough to tell others," said Loftus.

"Whether that is the truth or not, it will make no difference," said Hartley. "I don't particularly want your blood on my hands, but if either of you try to stop me getting away, you will be shot."

Julia began: "Father—"

"Don't interfere!" snapped Hartley.

He began to pull out the drawers of his desk and took papers from them. Loftus and Mike looked at the burly figure of Mrs. McFarlane and wondered how far they dare go. In both their minds one thing was certain; they must not allow Hartley to get away. Just what Loftus had stirred up they did not know, but it was clear that Hartley had been ready for this emergency.

Mike glanced at Loftus, who raised an eyebrow. Hartley appeared to notice nothing, while Mrs. McFarlane stood in the doorway, the gun unwavering.

"Ah—here they are!" said Hartley with an air of pleased surprise.

He took a small box from the drawer, opened it, and extracted something which Loftus could not see. He looked round, smiled, and flicked one of the contents at Loftus, so that they jumped to their feet—and Mrs. McFarlane snapped:

"*Sit down!*"

"It will do you no serious harm," said Hartley easily. "Errol has already had a dose." He smiled broadly, and Loftus and Errol saw the smile widening, saw his face begin to get vague, and realised that they could do nothing to keep themselves awake, nothing to prevent Hartley from escaping.

Three of Craigie's men saw Sir Basil Hartley walking about the grounds of Lyddon House while Loftus and Mike were inside, and the same three saw Mrs. McFarlane in the back garden. Hartley exchanged a courteous greeting with two of them, and a moment or two afterwards each man felt the sharp pinprick which Loftus had experienced. The third man, who did not know that Hartley saw him, thought that he had picked up a thorn from a wild rose.

Within three minutes all three were unconscious. They were the only men at the house.

No one saw what happened to Hartley and Mrs. McFarlane after that, and it was more than an hour before the alarm was raised. That was when Loftus, sufficiently recovered to reach the telephone, put a call through to Miller, and then dropped the telephone and slumped back in his chair. He saw Julia sitting back by the typewriter with her eyes closed; a little dart was sticking in her right cheek.

He began to feel better soon afterwards, and the others stirred. The dose was small—nothing like so much of the drug could be administered by the darts as by a hypodermic syringe. By the time he was on his feet again, Loftus admitted that there was nothing exceptional about what had happened; barbitone and kindred drugs worked just as quickly. It served simply to prove that Hartley had been well prepared.

By the time the police arrived, together with Hammond, who had been working with Miller that day, all of the victims felt better. Julia seemed to be dazed, much as Pamela had been when Mike had first seen her.

Loftus left the talking to Hammond. Julia could only keep repeating that she knew nothing of what was behind it—she had been as astounded as Loftus.

They found nothing to help them at the house.

They were on tenterhooks for word from Pitt, who had followed Fergus Grey away from the Hartleys, but it was dark before the agent telephoned to the house. Loftus was nearest the telephone, and he said quickly:

"Yes, go ahead—where is Grey?"

"Back at the pub," said Pitt in a blank voice. "I followed him nearly as far as Guildford, and then he came back to Woking, went into the pub and straight up to his room. I've got my eye on the stairs now, and I managed to get a local Robert to watch the window. Do you want him?"

"I'll come over," said Loftus.

He went along, leaving Mike and Hammond to continue looking through Lyddon House. All of them were feeling the shock of Hartley's complicity.

The first glimmering of the bewildering possibility that Hartley was concerned had come to Loftus when he had been talking with Hershall; he had seen the chance of a clever ruse to make it seem that Hartley was quite innocent. The idea had come and gone quickly, and afterwards he had fought against thinking it likely, because he could see no reason for it. He still could not see what was behind it, but when Grey had behaved so strangely and Hartley had refused to admit that "Mandino" meant anything to him, he had lost no time in acting.

"And Hartley reacted beautifully," Loftus said to himself as he walked laboriously up the stairs of the Gorse and Briar. Pitt was downstairs, watching the front door, and other men had been stationed near the inn, to make sure that Grey did not get away.

Yet with everything Loftus now had a sense of uncertainty. In the darkness especially, one of those little darts could be used without warning, and one would be enough for each man. He had an eerie feeling that Brenn, Witherspoon and Hartley could do exactly what they liked.

Grey looked a complete wreck. His expression was haggard, his hair stood on end, and his collar and tie were off. There was a strong smell of whisky in the room.

"Wha—what do—do you want?"

"Just a few words with you," said Loftus, quietly. He went in and perched himself on the arm of an easy-chair. "We haven't questioned you before because we thought it could hang fire. Carruthers knew you and vouched for you"—that was a half-lie which would probably have some effect—"and we thought that before long you would tell us all about it. Instead, you wander about Woking half-drunk most evenings, and you're getting deeper and deeper into the mire. You're scared of Brenn—"

"So would *you* be!" Grey broke off abruptly.

Loftus said: "Listen to me, Grey. I have direct instructions from a high Government authority to get to the bottom of this business. If you can give us information, but don't, the responsibility would be more than I would care to have on my shoulders."

"You can't bluff me," said Grey thinly, but he looked curiously at Loftus, as if trying to read his thoughts. "This is a crooked business, I know, but—"

"It's more than crooked. I don't know how big it is, but the stakes are very high. Hartley is a member of an important Commission which has been attacked by Brenn and Witherspoon. Several high Government officials have been blinded."

"Are you—serious?"

"Yes," said Loftus, emphatically.

"It—it doesn't make sense!" snapped Grey. "It's a miserable business as far as I'm concerned, but it can't go any deeper than—than—" his voice trailed off, and Loftus followed up his advantage quickly.

"It's so deep that Hershall himself has taken an interest," he said. "And we're getting fairly near. I accused Hartley of complicity in it after you'd seen him, and he ran away."

"Hartley did?"

"Yes. You and I between us managed to throw a real scare into him," said Loftus, "and he's disappeared. For a start—why did you warn him about Mandino? What do you know about Mandino?"

Grey drew a deep breath, turned and poured out a tumbler of whisky; his hand shook, but none of the whisky spilled. He took a gulp of the neat spirit, choked, and then stood with the glass in his hand, swaying unsteadily on his feet.

"All right—you win." There was a savage note in his voice. "I was working with the Mid-Southern Synthetics Company, which is one of the smaller combines. Brenn held a lot of its stock—anyhow, he had a big interest. We had a brilliant research man, who worked out something for economising on costs—it was good. You don't want technical details, do you?"

"No."

"This thing was good," repeated Grey. "It would have cut down costs by thirty per cent, if not more. This fellow—named Garnett—told me about it. He was a bit worried. In law anything a man invents, while employed by anyone in the same line of business as the invention, belongs to the employers, not the inventor. Often satisfactory arrangements can be made between the two parties, but Mid-Southern weren't likely to be helpful at that time. Garnett asked me if I could put some money up, so that he could resign, and then come across with the invention afterwards. Is that clear?"

"Very," said Loftus, eyeing the man intently.

"I hadn't any money, but I thought I could get some from my uncle. The whole estate *ought* to have been mine," he added, bitterly. "You've probably heard something about that, but it makes no odds—he wouldn't take any interest, and he wouldn't do anything to help me. That's when we first quarrelled really violently. Well, I didn't know who else to approach, but, the same night, *Brenn* approached me."

"Under that name?"

"Yes. I didn't know who he was then. I believe he was a director of Mid-Southern under a different name. Anyhow, he asked me whether I knew what Garnett was doing, and how much Garnett would sell the invention for. I'd gone on a blind after seeing my uncle, and I talked too much. I made that invention sound just as big as it was—and Brenn offered five thousand pounds for it. Garnett wouldn't sell. Garnett," went on Grey, slowly, "was murdered two days afterwards, and his drawings and documents stolen. Brenn killed him—oh, it looked like an accident, it never reached the police courts, but it was murder, and I knew it. Brenn bribed me. He paid me the five thousand for saying nothing—or so I thought! Actually, once I'd taken the money, he had me where he wanted me. I passed on a lot of odds and ends of technical information, although they weren't mine to pass on, and I got myself into a hell of a mess. I—I don't mind admitting that I was scared out of my wits," Grey added, and then took another gulp of whisky. Gasping, he snapped: "And I've been scared ever since!"

"That's not surprising," Loftus said, quietly.

"You're the hero type; you don't know what fear is," said Grey, with a sneer in his voice. "Oh, I know! Well, Brenn didn't worry me so much for a while afterwards, and I thought things were settling down. Then, about three years ago, I had a visit from Mandino. He—he had just lost his sight."

Loftus said: "Go on, Grey."

Grey stared at him blankly and was silent for a long time, but he continued at last.

"He knew Brenn had something on me, and he asked for my help. In return he said that he could persuade my uncle to change his attitude towards me. I was pretty sozzled most of the time, and I took a lot of risks which I wouldn't have done if I'd been sober. What Mandino wanted was evidence which would convict Brenn of murder, or of a crime to put him inside for a long spell. I was willing to co-operate, but I wanted more information about my uncle's position. I don't know what Mandino had against him, but I do know that he could make uncle do whatever he said. That didn't improve the relationship between me and Uncle Basil," he went on, "and Julia knew there was something going on which she didn't know about. We'd been pretty good friends until then, and I think she would have been more friendly if I hadn't been such a soaker. Anyhow, things cooled off between us. Uncle was getting more reasonable and even promised to give me a part interest in the estate. Then Mandino backed out. I didn't know why at the time, but Brenn told me all about it afterwards. Mandino's daughter was kidnapped. He worshipped her, and he went all to pieces when she was in their hands. He believed that Uncle had something to do with it, and he always said that the time would come when he would get even. That's why I went to report this afternoon."

"Why did you warn Hartley?" Loftus asked quietly.

Grey swilled the whisky round in his glass, and then said defiantly:

"What would you know about it? Have you seen Julia and him together? She—well, she worships him as much as Mandino worshipped Pamela. I got to know Pamela a bit, and I didn't blame Mandino, but—well, I'm in love with Julia! D'you get that? I'm in love with her! I wanted to try to help her."

Loftus spoke after a short pause.

"Grey, what has Brenn asked you to do recently?"

Grey did not answer.

"It's something to do with Julia, I suppose?"

Grey stiffened and turned round.

"So you've got the wit to see that," he sneered. "Yes, it's something to do with Julia. He wanted me to help to frame her for some crime or other. Julia is as straight as they come. Brenn had her father where he wanted him, and made Hartley help whenever he wished, but Julia stood between Brenn and the man, up to a point. Brenn hadn't the same control over her, and he wanted it—it's no use asking me why. Anyhow, I wouldn't play ball. Brenn used a lot of threats, and it got me down, but he didn't make me do anything."

"I know," said Loftus, smiling. "I've heard all about your last interview with him. It's quite a tangle, isn't it?"

"I didn't say that I could explain it."

"You've explained a lot," Loftus said, "but there is another thing—why did you go to Lyddon House, on the night your uncle went blind, and pretend to be drunk? And why did you sneak out of the house?"

"I went in that way because it was the only condition in which I even stood a chance of being allowed to stay," said Grey. "I had seen Brenn, and I thought he was brewing something up for Uncle Basil and Julia. I went to warn them. Then I gathered that something had gone wrong—I didn't know what, but that didn't matter. And your man, Errol, was on the premises. He saw through my acting. It wasn't any use my talking, anyhow. I could have warned Hartley, but with him out of action anything I said would imply that I had had something to do with it. So I kept quiet. Believe it or not," he added abruptly, "that's the truth!"

"Right!" Loftus spoke briskly and stood up. "Thanks, Grey. I've told you that Hartley has cleared off, haven't I? Julia's at the house alone, and I imagine that she's feeling pretty rough. How long will it take you to sober up?"

Grey stared at him, his eyes narrowing; and then slowly he began to smile.

Mandino listened gravely to what Loftus said as Loftus talked of his association with Sir Basil Hartley and what Grey had told him, while Pamela sat in an easy-chair opposite her father. Mike Errol was still at the Guest House, but Hammond had gone to London. The Dales were upstairs in Carruthers' room.

"How much of it is true?" Loftus asked finally.

"I think the whole story is true," said Mandino. "At one time I could make Hartley do whatever I liked. You see, he was never a particularly honest man, and as an accountant—before he called himself an economist and became *Sir* Basil—he had faked some accounts, very large figures, for the Mid-Southern Company. A word from me would have ruined him—I'm afraid I am admitting to an illegal attitude, Loftus, but you know something of the circumstances. I was *always* seeking a way of avenging myself on Brenn—or, before the time when I wanted vengeance, I was looking for a way of making sure that he did not best me. I knew that Hartley and Brenn worked together, but I don't know what they have been doing of late. I wish I did."

Loftus did not know quite what to make of the blind man, and although he believed that Pamela's curious history was genuine, he could not take that for granted.

He set into motion an inquiry into the board of the Mid-Southern Synthetics Company, and then he came to a full stop, for the company had some years ago been the subject of a take-over bid. Its directors had changed and its staff had been merged with the parent company.

He had an uncomfortable feeling that the next move would come from Brenn, and he felt quite helpless to prevent anything the man wanted to do. The need for finding out exactly what he was planning grew more urgent with every passing hour.

Wearily, Loftus cleared up some desk work late that night before going to see whether Craigie was still up.

14

INNOCENT VICTIMS

The seven members of the night-staff at the Mid-Southern Company who died that night had no idea that Brenn planned their death. They went to work, as usual, with others of the night-shift.

The explosion came, it was said afterwards, from the boiler-house.

There was no warning; one moment several dozen men in drab overalls were working quietly, using their tools expertly, and the next there was the roar of the explosion, a sudden horror of steam and flame and smoke and crashing machinery, the shrieks of men and women, the hiss of running water, the grinding noise as machines began to fail and great wheels slowed down. Falling masonry added to the chaos, and it was some time before those who survived, and those outside the immediate scene of the explosion, began to pull themselves together to start the work of rescue.

Next day, Loftus, brooding, and waiting for a call from Hammond, who had spent the morning with Julia Hartley, glanced down the back-page columns of the *Evening News*. One of the agents had left it on the desk.

SEVEN DIE IN BOILER EXPLOSION
Cause Unknown

He would not have read further but for the name which caught his eye—the Mid-Southern. He scanned the item quickly, his eyes narrowing. He read it again, but could only glean that there had been an explosion and that seven people had died. He put in a call to the Yard immediately, and was promised information as soon as possible.

Hammond rang through soon after; he was unable to get any information, and he believed Julia meant it when she said that she had no idea where her father might be. Loftus passed on the Mid-Southern item and replaced the receiver as another telephone rang. He lifted the receiver and, to his surprise, heard Christine's voice. It was an unwritten rule that when anything was afoot she would only telephone the office in real emergency, and he was not surprised to hear the note of excitement in her voice.

"Bill, I had to ring you—I've just had a call from Brenn!"

"Have you, by George!" said Loftus. "And what does the little gentleman have to say?"

"He said: 'Loftus had better stop, unless he wants a repetition of the Mid-Southern incident in many other places. We have been very patient,'" Christine said breathlessly, and went on: "It was right to call, wasn't it? And, Bill, what incident does he mean?"

"A little explosion," said Loftus, "I'll tell you all about it later. He said nothing else?"

"No."

"You tried to get the call traced, I suppose?"

"Yes, but I couldn't get any information except that it was some-where in London."

"For all we know he might be living next door," growled Loftus.

"What beautiful ideas you do have," said Christine, and then added, laughingly: "Good-bye, darling—be good!"

Loftus laughed as he rang down, but he was not laughing for long. He did not think Brenn was bluffing, and he believed that he was directly responsible for the accident at the Mid-Southern Company works. The threat of repetitions was probably serious also.

He was even more puzzled.

The ability to cast the spell of blindness, that hideous discovery which Witherspoon had made, was surely enough to enable Brenn to work without such incidents as the boiler-house explosion. For the first time, Loftus experienced a rise of hope; it might be that Witherspoon had come to the end of his supply of the drug. There had been no outbreak of the plague for several days, and now this suggested that Brenn was falling back on his second line of defence.

It was possible that Brenn meant Loftus to understand that innocent victims would suffer, and that the blindness was reserved for people of consequence. That was a disquieting thought.

He got in touch with the Home Office and had some difficulty in convincing the official whom he first approached that he was serious, but the name of Hershall succeeded in gaining him a hearing. He suggested that all factories mentioned in the list which Mandino had given him should be specially guarded and that other places not on the list be told to take special precautions. It was not until late evening that he succeeded in getting his way, and the messages were sent out; they did not prevent two further explosions, one in the Midlands and one in South Wales. The death-roll was lighter—five died altogether—and the damage was not extensive.

Craigie came to the office the next morning.

At half-past ten the telephone rang and Loftus heard Christine again—and this time her voice was strained.

"Brenn?" asked Loftus sharply.

"Yes," said Christine. "And the message was practically the same as yesterday."

"What *is* he doing?" Loftus demanded after he had replaced the receiver and was looking at Craigie, who leaned back in an easy-chair and puffed steadily at his pipe. "Why the complete switchover? Three places affected, all on the list which Mandino supplied—but, *why?*"

Craigie said slowly:

"Bill, I think I'm beginning to see a glimmering of an idea—I haven't been lying back and thinking for no purpose at all!" He sat up and stared towards Loftus, who was so intent on his words that for once he missed the poignancy of looking into Craigie's sightless eyes.

"Go on," said Loftus.

"Supposing Brenn, for some reason or other, has been trying to make us concentrate on one thing while he is really after another?"

"Ah," said Loftus. "I've toyed with the thought, but I've never been able to give a good enough reason for it."

"Assume there is a sound reason," said Craigie. "Where is the evidence that he's been working so? Give me your observations and I'll see how they link up with mine."

Loftus regarded him soberly for several minutes. Craigie refilled his pipe, and no one who did not know what was the matter with him would have dreamed of his affliction. The room was remarkably silent until Loftus said:

"In the first place, take Mike. After all those preparations they virtually let him go. In the second place, Pamela Mandino. After keeping her for three years, according to the evidence, they let her go even more easily than Mike. Curious, to say the least."

"Well," said Craigie, slowly, "we're both starting from the same place."

"Good! From the beginning, were they taken in by Mike or did they deliberately let us think that they were? Did they go to enormous lengths to convince us that he was going to work for Brenn, only to be allowed to escape so that he could come and tell us what he did, and to pass on all he knew about Mandino? Again, Brenn has proved himself cunning above the average, yet he allowed Carruthers to hover about on the common and even give him a lift to London. It just doesn't add up with all we know of Brenn. There are several other pointers, the most important being, as far as I can see, that he deliberately gave us Mandino's name, he deliberately persuaded us to go after Mandino, and once we'd got to the house he went to extraordinary lengths to make us think that Mandino could give information of value. Is that so? Are the names and addresses of these firms really of any use, or has Brenn finished with his interest in them? Is he making us look along those lines, and arranging these infernal accidents to make doubly sure that we think we're on the right track?" Loftus was speaking very swiftly, and Craigie was looking towards him, his face expressionless. "I would say, 'yes,' to all the questions if I could only see the reason," Loftus went on. "Take the Hartley business: Hartley was absolutely thrown at us. It was known that we were interested in him, so he was blinded and then made well again—could that be because they wanted to make sure that we turned our attention to Hartley? Then there's Fergus Grey. On his own admission he's scared of Brenn. Has Brenn forced him to pitch the story he gave me—perhaps it's true in many respects, but with important omissions—to keep us harping on the same business? Gordon, if I'm right, if it's a gigantic red-herring, what is behind it all?"

Craigie said: "If this is a gigantic effort to bluff us, we have to look at the people who are supposedly free from suspicion."

Loftus leaned against the mantelpiece.

"Don't tell me—I know! Mandino, Pamela, Julia Hartley, Fergus Grey. None of them measure up except, possibly, Mandino."

"I've had an idea about Mandino," said Craigie.

"What is it?"

"Is he really blind?" asked Craigie quietly. "Yes, I know it sounds fantastic, but we ought to make quite sure. I think Mike can check up on that as well as anyone, and he's the most likely man to be at the Guest House. Will you get him busy?"

"Yes," said Loftus, "I certainly will!"

They had had dinner together in the charming dining-room at the Guest House. The Dales had managed to get all their other rooms empty, since they had been assured that any loss would be made up by the Department, and so the party consisted of Mandino and Pamela, Mike, Carruthers—who was now beginning to feel the real-isation of what had happened, but made a good effort to conceal his frequent periods of depression—the Dales themselves and, because an opportunity had presented itself, Julia and Fergus Grey. In view of everything that had happened it would not have been surprising had there been some gloom at the table, or at best a brittle gaiety. Instead, everyone seemed normal and reasonably happy.

Mike was intrigued by the Julia-Fergus Grey *rapprochement*. Loftus had told him the position between the couple, and he had found that Grey was spending a lot of time at Lyddon House and the cousins appeared to be getting on well.

For two days Mike and the Dales had watched Mandino closely, and nothing at all that he had done suggested that Loftus might be right. True, he moved about with remarkable certainty and did many things for himself which Carruthers could not do; in spite of the loss of his servant, Polly, he got along very well.

Polly's charred body had been found in the ruins at Tynham Place.

Mike himself was feeling deflated. He had secretly believed that if he could bring Fergus Grey and the Mandinos into the house together they would give something away, and so explain more fully Pamela's reaction when she had seen Grey and Grey's when he had seen the Mandinos. They had recovered from the shock of that first encounter, however, and behaved like old acquaintances pleased to pick up the threads of friendship.

The unnatural thing to Mike was the naturalness of everything.

Mike was more proud of the Department than he was of himself. He came to the conclusion that he was putting up another poor show, and did not realise that unwittingly he was playing a not insignificant part in finding the real motive behind the crazy series of crimes.

The first intimation came when there was a telephone call, which he jumped up to answer, as he was nearest the door. It was Loftus, and the only thing that appeared to materialise was yet another fantastic twist in the sinister business.

"Is that the Guest House?" asked Loftus, sharply.

"Yessir," said Mike, intending to be humourous.

"What the devil—" began Loftus, and Mike heard him draw in his breath. "Mike, is that *you?*"

"I should be surprised to find it isn't," said Mike, mildly. "Don't I sound like myself?" When Loftus did not answer immediately, Mike went on: "Don't I?"

"Be quiet a minute, and let me get over this," said Loftus. Mike held on, frowning, until Loftus began to speak again more normally, but with a wondering note still in his voice. "Listen, Mike, Brenn came through on the phone a few minutes ago and said that you wouldn't get away so easily this time. I thought something had gone wrong down there."

"Everything is as peaceful as could be," said Mike. "More bluff by Mr. Brenn, I suppose?"

"He didn't give me the impression that he was bluffing," said Loftus.

Mike said sharply: "Where's Mark?"

"That's just what I'm beginning to wonder," said Loftus, slowly. "They may have picked him up in mistake for you. He was keeping an eye on the St. Albans house. Come up at once, will you?"

"Yes," said Mike, and he replaced the receiver and stared grimly at the whitewashed wall of the cupboard before going to tell the others that he had been called away.

Seen together there was no difficulty in distinguishing Mike Errol from his cousin Mark, although people who saw them for the first time were often confused. When apart they were often taken for each other, although on Department work they usually shared the same assignment.

Mark was a shade darker than his cousin, he dressed a little more carefully, and his face was more often without a smile. His voice, too, was brisker, but there was so little difference that it was not surprising that he was mistaken for Mike that evening as dusk was falling.

He was *au fait* with all that had happened, and knew the story of the St. Albans house. One of the many amazing things in the affair had been the ease with which Brenn and Witherspoon had deserted that house when Mike had escaped. Mark, who had a curious turn of mind, went to the exit which had been discovered in the meadow, and looked through the barn—once used as a garage.

He knew that Brenn himself had bought the house, many years before, under the name of Crow, and he had made many inquiries about the occupants of the house from the neighbours. He found that no one knew a great deal about Brenn or Witherspoon, but the occupants of the houses on Hill Top Rise made a habit of keeping themselves to themselves, and all the neighbours knew very little about one another.

Mark sauntered about the barn.

He had the electric light on. There was no shade, and the garish light showed up the odds and ends of equipment, the small bench fastened to one side of the wall, and the spare tyres hanging from rafters. Looking at the tools on the bench, he saw a small tin of oil lying on its side, and as he stretched over to right it he knocked a spanner to the earthen floor. Bending down to retrieve the spanner, he saw a curious thing: a strip of glass about a foot long and two inches wide, set in the wall beneath the bench. As far as he could see, it was fitted from the outside.

He went out.

One side of the barn was supported on wooden blocks, the other was actually built into the sloping ground. There was nothing to indicate the glass panel; obviously it was built beneath the earth. He was excited as he went nearer, but he could find no way of getting to the window. He returned to the barn, examined the glass again, and this time he saw that there were the outlines of a trapdoor in the wall of the barn, cleverly concealed by the wood of the bench.

He repressed a temptation to investigate on his own, and went out to summon another man who was also watching the house; Loftus had prepared for the possibility that Brenn or one of the others would return to reconnoitre the place.

Mark was half-way across the meadow when a man appeared *out of the earth*. It happened so swiftly that he had no time to get his gun or to shout; a large piece of turf was pushed up and a man jumped up almost in his path and struck at him with a cosh. It caught him on the side of the head and sent him reeling. A second blow, delivered with more precision, knocked him out; he was lifted bodily, carried a few yards, and then pushed through a hole in the ground. From there he was carried along a narrow tunnel which led to one very similar to that which Loftus and the others had already discovered; it actually ran parallel.

He came round half an hour later in a room which was well lighted, well-ventilated, and pleasantly furnished. Although he had not seen Brenn in person—he had seen Witherspoon in London—he did not doubt the identity of the man who was sitting in an easy-chair and looking at him. He himself was stretched out on a settee, and the light hurt his eyes.

Witherspoon sat on an upright chair at a large bureau.

"Well, Errol?" said Brenn.

Mark pressed the tips of his fingers against his head.

"You shouldn't have come back," said Brenn, "you should have been satisfied with one piece of luck; you won't get away again. I've already told Loftus so."

"Oh," said Mark.

He was glad that he had every excuse for looking dazed, for the greeting startled him; then gradually it dawned on him that he had been mistaken for his cousin.

"This time you're here until you die," said Brenn. "You thought you were smart, Errol, but"—he laughed sarcastically—"I knew from the first that you were one of Craigie's men. I wasn't taken in by Carruthers; it would take a lot cleverer men than you or any of your fine friends to catch *me*. You've told Craigie and Loftus everything you thought you learned, too. All you learned was what I wanted *you* to learn."

"Oh," said Mark, stupidly.

"A bit of a shock, isn't it?" said Brenn. "It's nothing to what you're going to get. Everything was a trick. I have guided the course of *all* Craigie's investigations, while he thought he was so clever! I have foxed him, foxed the Government, and got the situation just as I want it. The fact that the first four men whom we treated worked on that Commission was one of the most fortunate things that could have been, for *I'm* not interested in the new economic plans!"

"Aren't you?" said Mark, helplessly.

"I am not! You may live long enough to find out what I am after, but that remains to be seen. It depends on how you behave yourself."

Witherspoon turned from the bureau and said slowly:

"Have you amused yourself enough, Brenn?"

"I'll never have enough of laughing at Craigie's men," Brenn said, standing up abruptly. "Have you finished?"

"Yes," said Witherspoon. He stood up, his tall, angular frame nearly touching the ceiling, and looked at Mark. "I shall be glad when we can settle down and finish with all this," he went on, "it has been most difficult to concentrate. You can have all you want of the drug by to-morrow mid-day."

"As soon as that?" asked Brenn sharply.

"By to-morrow midday," said Witherspoon.

"Splendid," said Brenn very softly, "splendid, we can act by to-morrow evening, and then—and then—" He threw back his head and laughed uproariously, while Mark stared at him and wondered if he were sane.

A bell rang sharply.

Brenn stopped laughing so abruptly that it looked as if he had forced the laugh. The telephone was on a small table near the door. He lifted it and said:

"Yes . . . *who?*" He listened for some seconds and then said sharply: "All right." He replaced the receiver and looked at Mark, then glanced at Witherspoon. His manner was puzzling, and he did not speak for several seconds.

"Loftus is outside again," he said at last.

"Loftus!" exclaimed Mark, sitting up.

"If you imagine that he or anyone else will help you, you're mistaken," said Brenn, with a sneer in his voice. "They can't find us here."

"I came precious near it," snapped Mark.

He stopped as Brenn drew near him. He had heard of the use which had been made of the hypodermic syringe, but he sat rigid when he saw one appear in Brenn's hand. The man did not speak, but Witherspoon stepped to Mark and thrust his arm forward, pushing his sleeve up. Brenn plunged the needle in.

15

THE FORMULAE

Loftus stood on the threshold of the room where the floorboards had been taken up, and saw other traces of a visitation. In one corner of the room had lain the body of the agent who had been working with Mark Errol; it was now on the way to the nearest morgue. The agent had been murdered with a knife thrust to the heart from behind, as if he had been taken completely unawares.

Mike stood next to Loftus, and Hammond was on his knees beside one of the floorboards. There were many other men in the house, for Loftus had not come with small forces.

"Well, what do you make of it?" asked Loftus.

"It's pretty clear," said Mike. "They had something hidden here, and came back for it. I hope Mark—" His voice trailed off as he looked towards the corner where the other man had been found.

Loftus shook his head.

"No," he said slowly, "that's too obvious; it's another piece of the trickery which gives Brenn such a lot of amusement. Mark wasn't hauled off and Peter wasn't killed because the others wanted what was hidden beneath those boards."

"I'm inclined to agree," said Hammond, rising and dusting his knees.

"What, more swings and roundabouts?" asked Mike. "What do you divine from it?"

"That they're still near here," said Loftus, "and having grabbed Mark, who stumbled on something useful, they had to think up a plausible reason for what they've done. Not that it helps a great deal; 'near here' might be anywhere within a few miles radius. As far as we've been able to find out, Mark was last seen walking across the meadow, where a cowhand saw him."

"He'd be going to the barn," said Hammond.

"I wish it were daylight," said Loftus, "but let's see what we can find down there now."

They were half an hour in the barn before Mike, who went down on his knees to pick up a tool he knocked from the bench, noticed the glass window. He did more than that; he saw the top of a man's face, which quickly disappeared. He showed no change of expression, but stood up and dropped the tool on the bench. Then he lit a cigarette and said in tones of disgust:

"It's no go, Bill."

"There doesn't seem much," Loftus said, and then noticed the expression on Mike's face. He nodded and talked of trivialities as all of them went out of the barn. There was no moon and the night was pitch dark.

Loftus spoke softly.

"Don't talk until we can be sure we're not overheard."

They walked back, stumbling over the uneven ground, in what seemed like a disconsolate silence. Inside the house, Loftus led the way upstairs and went into a small bedroom. He sat on the edge of the bed and eyed Mike tensely.

"Well?"

"Glass window beneath bench, plus a pair of eyes," Mike said. "It wasn't imagination, either. I thought it would be better if I pretended to miss it, to give us time to have a real go."

"And you were right," said Loftus, softly. "This can't be another trick; we've got something at last." He glanced at Hammond, who was also on tenterhooks. "We'd better get the men placed round the barn and also round the house at once, so as to move as soon as dawn breaks. Anyone still at hand might try to get out, but they'll probably lie doggo for a while. If we start anything before it's light we'll defeat our own purpose."

"That's all right with me," said Hammond. "I'll get off on my rounds. We'd better send some cars away, hadn't we, to make it look as if we've given up?"

"Yes—or better still, send the men in them and have them walk back." Loftus was smiling towards Mike. "We can't be wrong this time," he added.

Waiting the five hours until dawn broke was not easy for any of them. The men were watching closely, straining their eyes to see if anyone moved in the darkness, starting at the slightest sound.

No alarm was raised.

Soon after five o'clock the first light appeared in the eastern sky, and the shapes of trees began to stand out against the grey. Cows in the fields began to move, dark, sluggish shapes; and the hedgerows awakened to life. Below, in the town, the movements of the early risers were audible; some lorries started off and went past the house; not long afterwards an Army convoy rumbled past.

Men materialised out of shadowy corners and from behind trees and bushes, but many more stayed hidden in case whoever was beneath the barn tried to get away. Loftus, Hammond and Mike, with two other men, actually approached the barn itself and went inside. That was as the light was getting brighter, and Loftus going down on his knees, saw the window.

Men were stationed near the bank of earth outside.

"Now let's be quick about it," he said.

Mike and Hammond used crowbars and levers to prise the bench from the wall. Tools clattered to the floor, oil spilled, the crash of rending wood made an ugly cacophony, but Loftus was intent only upon speed and did not mind what noise they made.

The bench came away and revealed the lines of the trapdoor built in the side.

"Be careful, now," Loftus said. "Gasmasks on, I think; they'll be up to anything."

Mike shattered the window, but nothing happened. He crashed an axe into the stout wood of the side of the barn and levered pieces out. Still nothing came from inside the hiding-place. The men outside were straining their eyes to notice any sign of movement, and straining their ears to catch the slightest sound, but the countryside about them seemed quiet and undisturbed.

"Room for one," Mike muttered, and pushed his way through the hole he had made.

He had an automatic in his hand, and saw someone moving not far along a narrow, lighted passage. He fired, heard a gasp, and saw a man fall. He also heard the clatter of something which he imagined was a sub-machine-gun. He could not stand upright, but as he hurried along the passage towards the man he had shot he saw that the bullet had struck him in the chest. His eyes were still open and Mike's mouth shaped in an O of surprise.

"Well, well," he mumbled, "the little undertaker!"

By the side of Jackman, the "undertaker," there was a sub-machine-gun. Mike picked it up and, with it nestled beneath his arm, he fired a few rounds at a door in front of him. The bullets carved a way through it, and the door sagged open.

Hammond and the two others were behind him and they found the door opened only into another narrow passage, in which there was room for them to stand upright. Another door faced them, and they went cautiously, expecting some form of attack, probably gas. They were right. Gas came billowing out of holes in the door. Mike thought that it was tear-gas, and thanked the fates that Loftus had instructed them to wear masks. Loftus was somewhere outside directing operations.

Mike reached the door.

It was of steel, and the machine-gun bullets made little impression on it, but they had carried a burner with them and began the work of forcing the door.

Mark Errol came round a long time after the injection.

He was still on the settee, and the light was still burning enough to hurt his eyes. As far as he could see, no one was in the room. He craned his neck and saw an open door. Voices were coming from the room beyond, and he heard the note of excitement, tinged with alarm.

"How many of them?"

"*Shoals* of them," said Witherspoon, "we shall be lucky to get away. Someone will pay for this!"

"Don't waste time talking," snapped Brenn. "Have you got all you want?"

"The formulae are in the bureau," Witherspoon said.

By then Mark was on his feet. He felt weak and his knees were unsteady, but he realised the significance of what he had heard, and he lurched towards the door. He would not have reached it in time had not someone burst into the room beyond, making Witherspoon turn round.

"They've got Jackman!" the man said, "and they're burning the other door down!"

"All right, Henry," said Brenn in a quiet voice.

Mark reached the door.

He could see into the other room; Henry's back was towards him, and neither Brenn nor Witherspoon was in sight, although he heard footsteps. He put a hand to the door, but it did not move easily. He saw Witherspoon come into sight, and exerted all his strength to close the door. An exclamation from Witherspoon was followed by a shot from Brenn, which struck the door as it gathered momentum and slammed home.

Mark heard a sharp "click."

He did not know that it meant that the lock of the door had gone home—it was self-locking—and that the others stood staring silently at the steel face of the door. From somewhere further away there came the noise of shooting. It was not from the direction of the heavy door, for Mark could not hear a sound from the next room.

He was not sure how long they would take to force their way in. He turned to the settee and dragged it to the door, then nearly fell on it. His forehead was beaded with perspiration, and he could hardly keep on his feet, but he managed to reach the two easy-chairs, wheeled them into position, and turned them on end. Even if the lock were forced it would be some time before Brenn and the others could get in.

He collapsed on a small chair, gasping for breath.

Nothing happened, except that he heard the sound of shooting from a long way off. He wiped his forehead, then ran through his pockets. They had taken everything, even his wallet. There was nothing he could use as a weapon.

He heard the thundering on the door and knew that they were fighting against time to get inside and to reach the bureau.

Mike Errol was the first to step through the door which had been opened with the oxy-acetylene burner. He went cautiously, still holding the tommy-gun, but there was no one in the big room beyond. The door at the other end was locked, but it was of wood. He fired at the lock, and as the door sagged open he went down on his knees. Shots were fired over his head and one of the men behind him was wounded, but Hammond, who had also dropped flat, was not hurt.

Mike fired a burst through the open door, and two men just inside the room went down. They had been pulling furniture to the door, and now it served as a barricade for Mike and Hammond. Another door beyond was open, and men were firing from it. All of them wore gas-masks.

It was some time before they could move on.

They did so at last, pushing the sideboard, which had been placed near the door, before them so that they could make progress while behind the cover of solid oak. The passage beyond was also well guarded, but a burst of machine-gun fire cleared it.

A heavy, banging sound reached Mike's ears.

The room beyond was L-shaped. The narrow end was out of sight, but it was from there that the banging was coming. Suddenly a man appeared—and Mike recognised Brenn's stocky figure.

Brenn went out of another door as a bullet struck the wall just behind him. Mike watched, tight-lipped, and as a second man appeared he got in a burst which brought the man down, but the drum of the machine-gun was emptied with the burst. When Witherspoon rushed across the far end of the room, Mike could do nothing to get him, and Hammond's shot just missed.

A door banged.

Mike and Hammond quickly climbed over the sideboard and hurried to the end of the room which the others had been banging. They saw the axes nearby, realised that a steel door had defied Brenn and Witherspoon, who had been trying to get it open until the last minute.

"That doesn't seem so bad," Mike said. "I wonder if Mark's around? Where's that burner?"

The man with the oxy-acetylene burner set to work.

Meanwhile, most of the men who were keeping watch outside were concentrating on the barn and the house itself. Nevertheless, several were keeping an eye on the meadow. Suddenly square blocks of turf in the meadow were pushed up, and men jumped from burrows in the ground and rushed towards the hedge and the road.

Shots were fired from several directions, but the men continued to run. Brenn and Witherspoon came in sight.

Witherspoon was slower than his partner, and lagged behind. Loftus, coming from the barn, saw and recognised him, and fired at his legs.

Witherspoon tripped up, and the bullet, which would have hit his legs, struck the back of his head. Loftus saw him fall, and hurried as swiftly as he could towards him, while one party maintained the chase after Brenn, Henry and the others. Not far away was a thick copse; beyond it an old Roman amphitheatre with several buildings a few yards away. The men with Brenn raced down the grass banks, across the middle of the theatre, and up the other side. One of them was hit by a bullet and fell backwards, but the others went on and disappeared among the trees. The search went on for a long time, but there was no further sign of Brenn or Henry or the other men who had escaped—five in all.

Witherspoon was dead, and four others, including Jackman, were either dead or badly wounded.

Later, in the lounge where Brenn had been so sure of himself, Mark sat in a state of exhaustion which was rapidly easing, thanks to a tot of whisky from Mike's ever-ready flask. He was watching Loftus and Hammond as they went through the papers in the bureau—among them, Mark had said, Witherspoon had left the formulae.

The underground premises revealed some surprising things. There was a small workshop where a great deal of experimental work had been done, as well as a laboratory and a doctor's surgery. There was evidence that quite a number of people worked there, and Loftus was reminded of Brenn's statement at Chiswick: that his workpeople had lived in the other houses in Tynham Place.

It was now quite certain that Brenn employed at least fifty or sixty men.

The fact that they had unearthed the St. Albans premises might have justified Loftus in thinking that Brenn was on the run, but he was not really satisfied about that. On the other hand, they had made progress which at one time had seemed impossible, and, a little later, his spirits soared much higher.

That was when they found a packet of papers covered with hieroglyphics—Greek to them all, but they had no doubt that they had discovered what they wanted. But there was still a disappointment in store, however, for all the papers and several books were filled with entries in a code, and the code could not be found. In their present form they made no sense at all, and Loftus, after glancing through them, put them aside.

"A job for the cypher experts," he said, pushing his chair back. "I think we can say that it's been quite a day for us!" He beamed at Mike and Mark.

Mark said: "Bill, I've been so filled with excitement that I haven't told you what might be the most interesting part of the whole business. Brenn was boasting that he had put over a tremendous bluff, and I think the most significant thing he said was that it was a lucky thing the four members—no, the four men he first attacked—were members of the Royal Commission. Does that help?"

Loftus stared at him thoughtfully.

"It might help a lot," he admitted. "Yes, it might help a great deal. We thought he went for them because they were members of the Commission. It looks as if there was some other reason, and that strengthens the theory that they've put out a lot of red-herrings." He rubbed his eyes. "I don't think it's much use trying to concentrate now, we'll work it out when we've had a spot of shut-eye."

Actually, before he went to bed, he passed in all that he had learned to Craigie, and also saw that the books were delivered to the Cypher Department.

He was asleep on the bed in the Department office and undisturbed by the frequent ringing of the telephone, which Craigie answered, when a bell rang softly and the green light showed in the mantelpiece. Craigie walked slowly across the room, groped for the right press-button. The visitor was Hershall.

"Things are better, aren't they?" he said.

"I think we ought to get results soon," said Craigie, feeling for his chair and sitting down cautiously. "Sit down, sir." Hershall sat on the arm of a chair, his favourite position in the office, and Craigie went on to give him some idea of what had been found and what was now being done.

"I've reason to think that the four members of the Commission, the first victims, were made blind for some other reason than their work on the Commission itself. I've been making inquiries—can't move fast, of course, but three reports are through—about the other work the three men have done and are doing."

Hershall nodded approval.

"Will you take the written reports, or shall I outline them now?" Craigie asked.

"I have half an hour to spare," said Hershall. "Go ahead."

Craigie talked quietly.

"Mr. Jacob Bennett, the first victim, was on the Royal Commission because of his great knowledge of industrial conditions and his exhaustive studies on the labour problem. He was a speciality man, and had worked on nothing else for a number of years, mainly in plastics, of course. Then Professor Arnold Rigby, specialist in synthetic materials," said Craigie, "and also about the most brilliant man there is in this country—by George!"

"What is it?" asked Hershall, as Craigie stared at him in amazement.

"Parmitter, who was blinded in the Middle East, was out there to make a report on a new man-made material," Craigie said in a low-pitched voice. "So we have three men on synthetics. I can't imagine that Parmitter, affected so far away, was part of Brenn's effort to side-track us. It looks as if it's to do with synthetics, doesn't it?"

When Hershall had gone, Craigie sat back, his mind working over all the known facts.

Loftus was not awakened until Hammond arrived. He glanced across at the big man, grinned, and went over and pinched his nostrils. The gentle, rhythmic snoring stopped instantaneously and Loftus opened his eyes.

"What?" he said.

"It's time all good little boys were up," said Hammond, "and I want a spell on your bed, anyhow!" He put a kettle on, filling it from a tap at a basin built into the wall, and busied himself making tea. He had brought in some sandwiches and some cold tongue, and talked as he worked.

Hammond had been trying to find out more about the man Garnett, who had been murdered four years ago for the sake of his invention, which would revolutionise the production of synthetic and plastic materials.

No one had suspected that he had been murdered; his body had been found at the foot of a cliff in the Avon Gorge, not far from Wischester, the headquarters of the Mid-Southern Company. Evidence had been forthcoming to show that he had been low and depressed for some months before his death, and a verdict of "accidental death" had been returned. Hammond had looked up all references to him, while information had been telephoned by a man sent down to inquire into his work. He had been a clever scientist, although not considered brilliant; apparently only Brenn apart from Fergus Grey had learned about his invention.

"And Brenn had to learn about it from someone before he approached Grey," Hammond said.

"Brenn was a director of the company at the time," Craigie reminded him, "and directors do have a trick of hearing most of the rumours that get around. Whether Grey or Garnett—was Garnett the man's name?"

"Yes."

"Whether Grey or Garnett, then, said something carelessly and word reached Brenn, I don't know," said Craigie, "but it seems the likely explanation. We want Grey again."

Loftus nodded as he sipped a cup of strong tea.

"Yes," said Hammond, "although I doubt whether he can do more than give us an idea of what the invention was. If he'd known the details, he would have said so."

"He might not," said Loftus, "and I asked him to eschew technical details. No, it was *not* another mistake," he declared, emphatically, "it was deliberate; we've let them all run on a long leash, and we aren't doing so badly as a result."

Hammond grinned.

"Thanks to Brenn's big mouth. Where's Mike?"

"Gone to his flat with Mark—I don't think we'll be popular if we wake 'em up just now."

"Who's left down at the Guest House?" asked Hammond.

"Reggie Pitt, Pip Evans and about umpteen others, all of whom are waiting to complain emphatically that they aren't getting as much excitement as they ought to," said Loftus. "Shall we go to see Grey or bring him here?"

"There'll be more danger if he's brought here," said Loftus. "I imagine that as soon as they guess we've cottoned on to his part in it— or, rather, what he can explain about Garnett's invention—they'll go all out to get him. Rout Mike and Mark out," he added, "never mind how tired they are. Send 'em down to Lyddon House to take Grey from there to the Guest House. Then send word to Pitt and Evans at the Guest House; they need to be more on the alert than ever."

"I am not so sure that the trouble will come as quickly as that," said Hammond, "no one can divine what we've guessed."

"And what we've guessed might not be right," Craigie said.

The concentration of Department men in the Woking area that early afternoon exceeded anything that had been contrived before. They had one task—to keep their eyes open for Brenn, Henry or any other of the identifiable members of the Brenn organisation.

The Guest House itself was thickly surrounded by Craigie's men and some plain-clothes policemen, including Sergeant Whitehead, of the local station.

The lounge of the Guest House was excellently situated for a secret conference. It had been built on to the house, so that three walls were outside walls, and the fourth was separated from the next room by a passage. Thus it was possible to keep every wall watched and to make sure that no one overheard what was said. Above there was Mandino's room.

When Grey saw Loftus, Hammond, Carruthers and the Errols altogether—he had been upstairs talking to Martha Dale when the main party had arrived from London—he looked at them with his eyebrows raised.

"It's to be a full-powered conference, is it?" he said.

"We'll call it that," said Loftus, smiling. He was astonished at the change in Grey since he had seen him at the Gorse and Briar. Gone were the bloodshot eyes, the trembling hands and the nervous manner. He seemed in complete control of himself, and he had much more confidence.

"Well, what can I do for you?" he asked.

"We're going back a bit—to the Garnett days," said Loftus quietly. "We want everything you can remember about Garnett's invention; you can go into as many technical details as you like this time. Mark Errol knows enough about synthetics to be able to follow you."

"Oh," said Grey, frowning. "Look here, Loftus, there's no come-back, is there? You—er—you practically promised that if I told you all I could I needn't worry about what I did four and five years ago."

Loftus said: "If you give us all the information you can, your grateful country will be much too pleased with you to think about trying to punish you for anything you did under Brenn's influence! In any case, with that influence established there isn't a very strong case in law. You can take that as final."

"Thanks," said Grey. "Well—here goes."

Much of what he said in the course of the next half-hour was Greek to Loftus, Hammond and Carruthers, but the Errols, always of a scientific turn of mind, followed him clearly.

"Of course, I can't be sure that it would work," said Grey, "but if Brenn's been going to these lengths to make sure that he can do what he likes with the whole synthetics market, it looks as if there's something in it. Garnett told me what he claimed for it, but he didn't give me any essential details."

"You're quite sure that Garnett didn't give any details to anyone else?"

"He told me that he hadn't discussed it with a soul," said Grey. "I think you can be sure of that."

"Good!" Loftus stood up and smiled down on him. "I should warn you that Brenn might discover that you're quite a cog in the wheel, and he might have a shot at killing you. To try to make sure he fails you'll be protected as well as we can manage it."

"Oh, I'm not worried," said Grey, carelessly. "As a matter of fact, I'm so much on top of the world that I don't think anything would really worry me!"

He was cut short by a scream which came from somewhere inside the house. It rang through the room, and every man jumped to his feet. The colour drained from Grey's face as if to belie his words.

Hammond reached the door and flung it open.

Footsteps pattered on the stairs and a man's voice—Jim Dale's—was heard.

"What is it, Pam?"

Pamela Mandino was at the foot of the stairs. She looked terrified, and was gasping for breath. Her lips were working, and for some seconds she could not speak.

Hammond climbed over the banisters, so that he did not need to pass her on the stairs, and hurried to the first floor. Mike followed him, while Mark stood with Dale. The girl's breathing grew more laboured; she looked as if she had received a shock which had sent her into hysterics. As he hurried to Mandino's room, Mike was reminded vividly of the fact that she had admitted that for long periods she had not been quite right in the head.

Hammond pushed open Mandino's door.

The old man was sitting in an easy-chair. There was a volume of Braille on his knees, and his hands were resting on the arms of the chair in so natural a pose that the sight of his throat, cut from ear to ear, looked even more grotesque than it was.

16

THE DEATH OF MANDINO

"But for one or two queer things, I would say that he had killed himself," said Loftus, later that evening. "He might even have dropped the knife, which was on the floor by his side, and put his hands on the arms of the chair. You can't see by the photograph, but it's the most natural position imaginable. However, there are curious features. For one thing, he would hardly do it suddenly, while reading. For another, assuming someone else killed him and made him sit as if he had been reading so naturally, his hands should have been *on* the open Braille volume. Blind men read with their fingers."

Craigie nodded.

Loftus seemed to have forgotten that Craigie could not see. Actually he deliberately talked bluntly, believing it better that Craigie should not think his feelings were being considered too much. Both of them realised that the death of Mandino had brought them to a climax which was very nearly an impasse.

"I think we would be wise to assume that he was murdered and afterwards searched, and that the murderer placed him in that position," said Loftus. "There is one way in which someone could have got into the house without being seen—I hadn't discovered it before, and I feel pretty grim about it."

"How could it have been done?" asked Craigie.

"From a tree to the roof and then down a skylight," Loftus said. "The place is surrounded by trees, several of them within jumping distance. The skylight had been blacked-out permanently—dating, no doubt, from the war—and it was not noticeable from inside, but when Hammond went up on the roof he saw it at once. None of the watchers would see anyone climbing through the trees. The skylight had been recently opened, so—" he shrugged his shoulders. "That looks like it, don't you think?"

"Not necessarily," said Craigie.

Loftus growled: "Why not?"

"The question is, *why* was Mandino killed," said Craigie. "The way it was done doesn't matter so much, but the reason really matters."

"Not to mention who killed him?" murmured Loftus.

"That will come from the 'why,'" said Craigie. "Now, it's a curious fact that although he could have been killed before, they chose a time when it was more difficult to get in the house than any other. The precautions you've taken before were nothing compared to those taken yesterday. That's right, isn't it?"

"Yes," conceded Loftus.

"Yet it suddenly became imperative," said Craigie. "He had been at the Guest House for some time, and no attempt at all was made. Then suddenly they swooped."

"I still don't follow," said Loftus.

Craigie said: "Bill, you've given me a full description of the house. The lounge where you were talking jutted out, and Mandino's room was immediately above it. You've often heard that a blind man's hearing is much more acute than that of a man with all his faculties, and even since the past few days I can confirm that. Mandino was sitting up in that room, and he heard you talking. *Someone else knew that he heard it, and had to kill him.*"

"Now, come!" exclaimed Loftus.

"I'm not saying that there's no other possible explanation," said Craigie, "but I think you ought to explore the possibilities of what I've suggested."

"The house was empty, apart from the Dales!"

"You've already admitted that someone could have got in," said Craigie, with a smile. "Be consistent, Bill! And, remember, Grey must have had some idea of why he was wanted. Have you pondered over the remarkable change in him and the ease with which he and Julia Hartley are getting on? It's curious, to say the least. Have you checked up where she was this afternoon?"

"No," said Loftus quietly. "I can't believe—"

"Steady!" said Craigie.

Loftus stared, and then laughed.

"Sorry! I'm getting pretty naïve, I know, but Julia Hartley and a murder like that—no, the difficulties are too many; it doesn't tally with anything."

"Will you check up?" asked Craigie.

Uneasily, Loftus promised that he would.

Meanwhile Hammond had been working along similar lines to those which Craigie had suggested, and some inquiries had been made about Julia's activities that afternoon. She had been seen to leave the house, but had disappeared among the trees. Loftus admitted that it was a curious fact that both Hartley and Mrs. McFarlane—who had never been discovered—had disappeared with the same remarkable ease. Hammond had followed it up when Julia and Grey had been in another part of the house. On going through her wardrobe he had found a pair of badly torn woollen stockings stuffed in a corner; there were traces of pine needles in them. The trees near the Guest House were pines. A tweed suit, which she had worn that afternoon, also had some of the brown needles sticking into it. Hammond was reluctant to come to the obvious conclusion, but he went straight to the Guest House, where he and Loftus compared notes.

Carruthers and the Errols were also there, and all of them were as reluctant as Hammond and Loftus to believe that Julia was a party to it, but—

"If this were a straightforward murder investigation she would be under detention by now," Loftus said. "It looks as if we'll have to bring her in. The devil of it is that it also involves Grey."

Carruthers said quietly:

"You know, we still haven't got anywhere near the end of this business yet. Craigie might be right in saying that Mandino overheard what was said this afternoon, but is there the slightest reason why Julia or Grey should imagine that he would? If Julia and Grey are in it together, or even if she is in it alone and has been putting it across us nicely, how could she possibly guess that, all of a sudden, Mandino was going to hear something which would put him in a position to be more dangerous? Brenn had lost interest in Mandino! I can't see why it was suddenly revived, and I just don't believe that Mandino was killed for the reason you seem to think."

Loftus looked towards him.

"Well, we're receptive to ideas."

"Don't think me swollen-headed!" said Carruthers, with a smile. "I mean, first things first, and all that—*how* did Hartley and Mrs. McFarlane get away so easily?"

"Where does that come in?" asked Mike.

"You're not so good," said Carruthers. "They did get away with mysterious ease. You're assuming now that someone did get from Lyddon House to this place, after disappearing in the same mysterious fashion. I'm disagreeing, up to a point, and yet—the evidence is plain. Julia Hartley climbed a pine tree, and presumably one was climbed this afternoon. So she got here by the same mysterious means. In short—"

Mike gasped: "The *Guest* House!"

"I'm *very* fond of Martha," Carruthers went on, "and I'm on the way to hating myself for putting this idea up, but Jim Dale did know a remarkable lot about me, didn't he? And he and Martha have been most anxious to help, haven't they? In spite of the obvious risk. Now"—Carruthers began to tap his fingers on his cigarette-case—"at St. Albans, according to what I've been told, you had some pretty hot work in tunnel-building. There's nothing remarkable in that, and air-raid shelters have been an excuse before for some nasty subterranean hide-outs, but couldn't a similar arrangement be made here? I mean, is there an easy way from the grounds of Lyddon House to the grounds of the Guest House, and is there a large cellar, or something of the kind, beneath either or both houses?"

He stopped speaking.

The others stared at him in silence, and had he been able to see their faces he would have realised the sensation that his words created.

"Well?" he asked, after a pause.

"The Dales," said Loftus, in a wondering voice. "No, I can't see—"

"You're not yourself," said Hammond briskly. "It would help to explain the murder. It would—" he looked suddenly towards the door, stood up and stepped across to it. The others watched him, Mike and Mark turning and putting their hands to their pockets for automatics. Then Hammond opened the door, but no one was there.

He shrugged.

"Sorry," he said, "but I'm not very easy in my mind at the moment! Let's assume that Mandino was killed because he heard what we were talking about this afternoon. Let's assume that Dale killed him. We *have* to assume, also, that Dale overheard what was said. Is there any reason for thinking that he hasn't overheard us now?"

"How?" asked Mike, quickly.

"If that was a deliberate rhyme it was not funny," said Hammond, with a half-smile. The more acute the danger the more detached Hammond always became. "Supposing the house is wired up and that conversation in any room can be heard without trouble after pressing a switch? It's reasonable, isn't it?"

"It's so reasonable that it's making my spine go goosey," said Mike, looking about him. "If we're right—"

"It won't be so easy to get out as it was to get in," said Loftus quickly, "but there's one thing you people seem to have forgotten."

"What is it?" asked Carruthers.

"You have been thinking so much about the Dale angle that you've missed the obvious fact that there might be something beneath the Guest House or in the grounds which they *don't* know about," said Loftus. "There's hope for Martha yet!" He stood up, yawning, but the yawn was a little too deliberate to be convincing. "As a matter of fact, I think we've been talking a lot of bilge—we've done too much talking and too little doing in this business. I'm going to bring Julia in for questioning—or, better still, go there and see her. Will Grey be there as late as this?"

"No, he'll be at the pub," said Carruthers.

"Good! We can tackle him after we've heard what the sweet Julia has to say," said Loftus. "I'm beginning to feel that our reluctance to think the worst of her has been occasioned by her pretty face—and that won't do at all!"

"I'll come with you," Hammond said.

"I *started* on Julia," Mike said, spiritedly, "it's partly my show."

"We'll all three go," said Loftus. "Keep Carry company, Mark, will you?"

"Yes," said Mark, without arguing.

Loftus looked at them all in turn, mouthing the words: "Keep talking," and, when he was sure that they understood, he began to walk about the room, closely examining the walls. By standing on tip-toe he could see above the picture-rail, and at intervals he saw little slits in it. At one point a piece of the picture-rail had been screwed into the wall and covered with paint. He took out a knife, used a broken blade as a screwdriver, and took the piece off.

A length of electric cable lay revealed; a tiny microphone was next to it.

The others came up to inspect it, and Loftus whispered to

Carruthers of what he had found. Carruthers nodded, and looked disturbed, but he made no comment.

Loftus replaced the piece of picture-rail as the others continued to talk of the Julia-Grey angle. Loftus had switched deliberately to that, so as to mislead whoever might be listening-in. That all their conversation had been overheard was now established beyond doubt.

Loftus did not speak of it on the way to Lyddon House. He was preoccupied with the thought of Carruthers, who obviously feared that the Dales—Martha especially—were involved. Loftus had some idea of what Carruthers felt for Martha, but he was by no means sure that the obvious conclusion was the right one.

When he got to Lyddon House he spoke to several of the men still in the grounds, and told them to be more careful than ever, but he gave them instructions with a sense of impotency. The knock-out drug used could, if sufficiently well handled, put all of them out of action for quite long enough. If there were a connection between Lyddon House and the Guest House normal precautions, especially at night, would serve little purpose.

Lyddon House was in darkness.

It struck Loftus, Hammond and Mike as curious that Julia elected to stay there on her own, although it had been suggested that she should move. Why she had clung to the house was a mystery which might now be solved, but none of them at heart wanted to believe that she had been a party to the murder of Mandino.

She opened the door herself, shining a torch on to them, and obviously relieved when she recognised them.

"It does get a bit uncanny at night," she said as she switched on the drawing-room lights. She was in a dressing-gown of royal blue, and her hair was dishevelled as if she had been in bed, but she looked alert as she glanced from one to the other. "I—I suppose you've no news of my father?"

"No, Miss Hartley," said Loftus, heavily. "We have not come to discuss your father, but to discuss you. Why did you climb to the roof of the Guest House this afternoon?"

They knew in that moment that she had been there, for she stepped back and clutched at her throat, her eyes staring at them in sudden horror and alarm.

17

JULIA

She made a great effort to regain her composure, while Loftus stared at her with an unchanging expression. In repose his face was almost ugly, and his great bulk must have had a forbidding effect.

"I—I was there," she said at last. "But—"

Loftus snapped: "Why did you kill Mandino?"

"I didn't," she said, but there was no life in her voice, and now she evaded his eyes. "I got there and went into his room. He was dead then. I came back immediately. I didn't wait for anything else—I've never been so frightened."

"There might be a strong enough reason to justify your killing him," Loftus said, "but lies and evasions won't help you."

"I didn't kill him," she repeated, but she did not seem to mind whether he believed her or not. "I've told you just what I found. I knew that you were going to question Fergus. I—I've been afraid for some time that you thought he knew more than he's said. I thought you might be going to accuse him. And I knew I could get to the house. I thought if I could overhear what was said I would know better what to do."

"How did you get there?" Loftus demanded.

"This house is very old, you know." She drew in her breath, and then went on hurriedly: "There used to be a lodge in the grounds of the Guest House—it was pulled down long ago, but at one time there was a tunnel from here to the lodge. It wasn't used very much, but Fergus and I often played in it when we were children. You come out just inside the grounds of the Guest House amongst the trees. Long before the Dales took over the Guest House I was very friendly with the people who lived there, and as a child I often climbed the trees and got into the house through the fanlight. It was a joke." She spoke so lifelessly that the very word "joke" seemed out of place. "I did it again to-day."

"In spite of what you're telling us, it didn't occur to you to warn us earlier about the tunnel, or to say that it probably explains how your father got away?" Loftus' voice was hard.

Julia spoke with a sudden flash of feeling.

"I shall never do anything that might harm him!"

"On the whole, I don't think I've ever listened to such a farrago of nonsense," said Loftus. "You'll have to think up something much better than this, Miss Hartley."

"I've told you the truth," she said. "Mandino was dead. I think he had only just been killed when I arrived. I didn't stay. When Fergus came away, and was quite free, I realised that I needn't have worried. Nothing goes right," she added, wearily, "nothing goes right at all."

Loftus tried another tack.

"Why were you worried so much about Grey?"

"Do you think I'm altogether a fool?" she asked, still wearily. "Don't you think that I know you are watching him just as you are watching me—and just as you kept your eyes on Father all the time? Oh, I know! You've been friendly and helpful and pleasant, but any one of you was liable to become hostile and dangerous. It's been unbearable! I don't know *why* I was frightened for Fergus; I only know that I think you are suspicious of him. It worries me terribly."

"You've suddenly grown very fond of Fergus Grey, haven't you?" asked Loftus, slowly.

She said: "I have *always* been fond of Fergus, and I do not intend to discuss him any further! I have told you the truth, and if you don't believe it"—she shrugged her shoulders—"there's nothing else I can do."

It was Hammond who broke in quietly:

"Before we go on to anything else, Miss Hartley, who else knows of this tunnel between the grounds of the two houses? Yourself, Grey and—who?"

"I don't know for sure," she said. "Mrs. McFarlane knew of it, of course."

"Do the Dales?"

She looked surprised. "Not to my knowledge."

"Is there any way from the house to the tunnel?"

"Not to my knowledge," she said again. "There used to be, I believe, but it was blocked up before I ever saw it. I don't even know exactly where it is—it leads from one of the cellars, I suppose. I've always used the entrance from the grounds."

"We'd like to look in the cellars," said Loftus.

They went downstairs, Julia wrapping her dressing-gown more tightly about her, and letting Mike Errol lead the way. There was electric lighting and the cellars, used mostly for storage, were nearly empty except for coal and logs, as well as oddments of disused furniture. Several of the walls had been repaired fairly recently, and one or two of the repairs attracted Loftus' interest. Hammond wanted to know if there was a map or plan of the house, but Julia said she knew of none.

"We'll need a surveyor," Loftus said, off-handedly, "and we'll need these cellars watched until we get them properly inspected. You won't mind if we leave men down here, Miss Hartley?"

"Will it make any difference if I do mind?" asked Julia, with another flash of spirit. "I—*oh!*"

Her voice ended in a scream.

She was staring past Loftus and the others, who swung round and saw a trapdoor opening in the floor of the cellar where they were standing. They had missed it because of the dust and dirt. Mike and Hammond groped for their guns as they stood watching, but whoever was coming was not trying to take them unawares.

The trapdoor took some moving. Two hands appeared, and then, although they might have expected it, they were surprised to see the top of Fergus Grey's red head.

"Well, well!" murmured Loftus.

He went forward and helped to raise the trapdoor. Grey looked up at him with a grin, and said:

"Thanks! What a weight!" He let the door fall back with a bang, and a cloud of dust rose up. He coughed as he climbed to the cellar, covered in dust and slime, his hands black and his clothes torn; but with a look of triumph on his face.

"Two minds with but a single thought!" he said. "After Mandino's death I put two and two together—*someone* got into the Guest House, and I wondered whether they arrived from our place." He grinned. "So I thought of ye olde subterranean passage and explored it. I found a branch tunnel, and here I am. The main tunnel leading to the Guest House grounds has been used a lot lately, by the way; there are shoals of footprints! We're getting on, aren't we?"

"We're doing famously," said Loftus, dryly.

"I hoped to spring the tunnel as a surprise on you," said Grey, "but I should have expected you to get on to it. How we see life! And if there's one tunnel, why shouldn't there be two?"

"Why, indeed," said Loftus.

His words were lost, on the instant, in the roar of an explosion which knocked them off their feet without giving them the slightest warning. Julia was thrown against Loftus, who had the presence of mind to try to save her from a heavy fall. There was a fury of noise, growing rapidly louder and filling the cellar, which boomed and reverberated with it. Plaster fell from the walls, dust rose high, and as they drew in their breath it caught at the back of their throats and made them choke. They had no chance to speak or to do anything at all.

Above them there was chaos.

Lyddon House had been visible against the sky, and many of Craigie's men were looking towards it, knowing that Loftus and the others were inside: the watchers were more on the alert than ever. The flash came first, followed by the roar of the explosion; then Lyddon House began to crumble, as if it had been taken by a giant hand and shaken to pieces. Flames rose a hundred feet into the air, illuminating the billowing smoke and the trees around, many of them blown down by the force of the blast. First one wing of the house, then another, went crashing down, brick piled upon brick, stone upon stone; and all the time the noise seemed to increase and could be heard for miles. The fire could be seen twenty miles away, and the roar, as the wind nursed it, was audible at the Guest House and in Woking.

The fire revealed the full extent of the destruction.

Only two walls of Lyddon House were left standing, and they were already rocking perilously. The rest was just rubble. Mark Errol, who saw the fire from a window, with Martha Dale and her husband on either side of him, felt terribly afraid; he did not know that Loftus and the others were in the cellar.

Of the men in the grounds, many had been injured by the explosion, and others were already trying to clear away some of the debris, but it was clear that it would take hours, if not days, to get beneath it and to find out whether anyone remained alive.

Craigie was telephoned when the rescue work was well on the way, and it was his first intimation of the catastrophe. Mark spoke to him, and Craigie asked him to come to Whitehall. He needed someone there more often these days, and Mark understood what prompted the request.

Craigie immediately telephoned Christine.

She took the news well, as he had known she would. She had been in bed, and she told him that Pamela was asleep and seemed to have passed the crisis. The girl had not been able to tell Christine anything more than was already known. Relieved that Christine was able to keep steady, Craigie promised to let her know the moment there was any news, and then replaced the receiver.

Another telephone rang.

The little light that showed which one it was was useless to him; he lifted two receivers before getting the right one; then he heard Brenn's voice.

It gave him a shock, greater perhaps than it should have done. He had rarely known anyone outside the Department or the immediate members of the Government who knew the number, and he had assumed that Brenn had not known it before, or he would not have telephoned Christine.

"Craigie?" Brenn said, and went on before Craigie could answer: "You asked for what happened, you know."

"I think you have asked for more than you realise," said Craigie, quietly.

"*I'm* all right," said Brenn, and went on sharply: "Listen to me— do you ever want to see again?"

"I shall be able to see quite soon," said Craigie.

"You *think* so," sneered Brenn. "You've got Faversham working on Witherspoon's formulae, but what you don't know is that Witherspoon didn't leave the formula for the cure in the bureau; *I've* got that one." When Craigie did not answer he went on harshly: "You, Carruthers and a dozen or so others are doomed to blindness for the rest of your life! That's not a pleasant thought, is it?"

Craigie said: "There are greater troubles."

"It's easy to talk now," said Brenn. "Listen to me: I know that you're on to what it is, I know all about what has happened, but I don't think you've passed it on. Understand this, Craigie: if you do you'll never see again. Get this into your head, too; I have ample supplies of the drug. I can administer it without difficulty. I can use it on Hershall—yes, *Hershall*—and anyone else I want to. And I shall destroy the antidote whenever I think there's any personal danger to me. Do you understand?"

"Exactly what are you trying to tell me?" asked Craigie.

"I'm telling you that I've got you where I want you," said Brenn, "and you mustn't make any mistake about it. I'll do a deal with you on my own terms."

"What are they?" asked Craigie.

"I thought that would make you prick up your ears," said Brenn with a sneer, "but I don't propose to talk about it on the telephone. I'll be at Loftus' flat in two hours' time. You'd better be there. In case you think that you'll be able to prevent me from getting away, remember two things. I am not alone in this, and Witherspoon was not the only one who knew how to handle a situation. If I don't get safely away the antidote will be destroyed—the lotions already in being *and* the formula. Don't try any tricks this time."

He rang off abruptly.

Craigie replaced the receiver and looked blankly across the room. He ran his hands through his hair, hesitated, and then lifted another receiver. After five minutes, Hershall was on the other end of the wire.

Craigie told him briefly what Brenn had said.

Hershall, who was never called during the night unless it were a matter of exceptional importance, asked him what he made of it.

"I think Brenn realises that he is in a corner and thinks he might be able to come to terms," Craigie said. "I think his approach ought to be rejected, but that I should see him; he'll probably talk more freely if I do. I can temporise at first, and tell him that I have to report to you before any decision is reached."

"Yes, I agree with you," said Hershall, "but what personal precautions are you going to take?"

"I think I'll take a chance," said Craigie. "I don't think he would have suggested the meeting unless he were nearly desperate. His last hope now is that he will be able to reach a compromise. If he finds out that I have the flat closely watched he might not come at all, and he might not talk so freely if he does."

"All right, I'll leave it to you," said Hershall.

Craigie replaced the receiver, groped for a meerschaum, and then heard the little bell which told him that a mantelpiece light was showing. Mark Errol came in; Craigie recognised him by his voice.

"Hallo, Gordon!" Mark said, trying not to sound as dispirited as he looked. "I haven't lost any time." He sat on the arm of a chair and looked at Craigie, trying to get used to the fact that those shrewd eyes could not see. He had come by road from Woking, and his thoughts on the journey had helped to put the finishing touch to his depression. He had seen the debris at Lyddon House, and he did not think there was the slightest chance that any of those trapped would be brought out alive.

"What is it like down there?" Craigie asked.

"It couldn't be much worse," Mark said.

"Do you know what caused it?"

"No. Loftus and Carry had come to the conclusion that there was a way of getting from the house to the Dales' place," said Mark, and went on to explain what had been said. "Finally, Bill decided that Julia Hartley was the most likely murderer, and went to see her. I imagine that when she realised that he guessed what she was up to she blew the damn place up. I've arranged for the whole neighbourhood to be closely watched, of course, but in the darkness and with thousands of people about—and there *are* thousands of sightseers— it's not going to be easy to prevent people slipping past."

"No," admitted Craigie, "but if there is another passage—"

"The grounds of the Guest House are well covered," said Mark. "I don't think we can do anything more than we are doing. I rather expect some kind of ultimatum from Brenn," he added, slowly: "It seems the logical course now."

"I've had it," Craigie said, "and I want you to hold the fort here until I've seen the gentleman!"

* * *

The agents of Department "Z" had Bill Loftus's word that Christine was a remarkable woman, and those who knew Christine were always ready to admit it. That night—actually it was a little after five o'clock in the morning, and the streets were already filled with a faint grey light—she proved it as she had never done before.

At the street door she greeted Craigie in a voice which held no tremor, led him up to the flat and to the small sitting-room, where she took him to an easy-chair and put a jar of tobacco and a box of cigarettes near him. Because meerschaums were not the easiest pipes to carry about, Craigie always kept one at Loftus's flat; Christine fetched one but did not offer to fill it.

"So you're going to see Brenn," she said. Craigie had telephoned half an hour before he had left.

"I think we're within sight of the end," he said.

"Yes. Bill would give his head to be here!"

Craigie smiled. "Bill has turned up so often when everyone thought him dead that I'm not assuming the worst now."

"I'm certainly not," said Christine. "Is there anything you'll want me for when he comes?"

"No." Craigie lit his pipe before adding: "How is Pamela?"

"I gave her some sleeping tablets," Christine told him. "They work wonders with her—she's still fast asleep." She seemed aware of the fact that she was talking a little for the sake of it, and added: "Shall I make some tea, Gordon?"

"It would be very welcome," Craigie said.

They were drinking tea when the front-door bell rang. Christine jumped up quickly enough to betray her edginess.

A moment or two later he heard Brenn's voice.

The man seemed to be alone. He greeted Christine briefly, and then walked heavily to the living-room. He stood on the threshold looking at Craigie, his face expressionless. Christine watched him, until he turned to her and said sharply:

"I shan't want you!"

He stepped into the room, and Christine closed the door. He

looked older, although Craigie did not know that. Much of the liveliness had gone out of his voice, and he had lost all the geniality which had proved so deceptive in the past.

"Before we start, Craigie," he said, "you've got to know this—if you don't accept my terms I'll do all the damage I can, and that will be a lot of damage. Do you understand?"

18

BRENN OFFERS TERMS

"Sit down," said Craigie.

Brenn hesitated, and then sat in an easy-chair, but he perched himself on the edge of it. Craigie could tell from the sound of his voice that he was the more nervous of the two, and he had no doubt that only desperation had driven the man here.

"Are you going to talk terms?" Brenn demanded harshly.

"I've had instructions to hear what you have to say, and to make a report," Craigie told him. "I've no authority to act."

"You carry a lot of weight," Brenn said.

"I'll use it whichever way I think best," replied Craigie.

He found himself in a curious position. Brenn was ill-at-ease, and he himself found it necessary to make him feel less on edge, to encourage him to talk! It was an ironic situation, and Craigie tried to get used to it as he said quietly: "I can tell you, Brenn, that we know you are planning to get control of the whole synthetics industry in this country."

"So you've guessed that," Brenn showed no surprise. "I am one of the syndicate which has worked on this for many years, and we mean to get what we've worked for. We're going to introduce new production methods and *we* are going to take the profit. There will be fantastic riches—riches beyond compare."

Craigie said: "There are pretty good profits now."

"We're not interested in small beer!" snapped Brenn. "We've planned this for a long time, Craigie. Out of what we make with the companies on which we start, we shall buy up others. First, we shall talk of our new methods, and by demonstrating we shall be able to get seats on the boards. Gradually we shall assume country-wide control. This isn't a dream; it has all been worked out in black and white. Synthetics will soon become the whole basis of the economy—clothing, furnishings, building even—and we shall control them."

"And then," said Craigie, when the man paused.

"You're not convinced," said Brenn, "but it's true, and nothing you can do will stop us! You were early to see that there was something behind the blindness; that was what you can call a new weapon—and is why we wanted it. Certain men—a very limited number—could understand the methods of production we propose to use, *if* they could see them. The only people who could have discovered what we were planning and perhaps have reported or even stopped it, were—" he drew a deep breath and went on: "Sir Basil Hartley, but he came on our side and is one of us; Jacob Bennett; Sir Douglas Salter; Arnold Rigby; Parmitter, now in the Middle East, and a number of others. Those who are most important have already been affected by the blindness, and others will be; we have it all thoroughly worked out. Even to-day we have agents in America who are going to put it into operation there. You see, Craigie, these men had to be prevented from *seeing* certain formulae which only they were ever likely to understand. It's easy to grasp now, isn't it?"

"Yes," said Craigie, quietly, "it is."

It was so simple and straightforward that it affected him oddly; he felt both numbed and chilled. They were planning to control the basic industry of the world so that, in time, they could dictate what terms they liked to industry and world trade.

The ramifications were so vast that he could not properly comprehend them. What he could understand was that Brenn had been right to say that he could make it a practical proposition. No matter how absurd the way he had worked, no matter what fantasies had been mooted, here was something which could be achieved—and was, in fact, on the point of maturity.

Brenn jumped to his feet.

"All right, Craigie! Now you know everything you want to know, and what good is it to you? If you don't do what we want it means blindness for you for the rest of your life, and we'll use it on every man who holds a key position we can reach. Don't make any mistake, Craigie, it can and will be done unless—"

"Unless what?" The man was mad, Craigie reflected.

"We want complete freedom to exploit our own discoveries as we wish," said Brenn, abruptly. "All talk of economic planning in the basic industries must go. The men who might be able to discover what formulae we use must remain incapacitated. We shall operate from somewhere unknown to you, but our representatives must be allowed freedom of movement and freedom of action. That's what we want, and that's what we're going to have!"

Craigie stared towards him.

Quite mad, he decided. If he were not, he would never put such a proposition, he would know that whatever the consequences no Government could accept dictation, and there could be no compromise.

Brenn said slowly: "Well, what about it?"

"I'll make my report."

"You and the others have twenty-four hours in which to make up your minds," said Brenn. "After that we'll start using our drug in earnest. If I don't get away safely now, if anyone tries to follow me, it will be started by the others. Get that clear, Craigie. If I'm not back where I'm due in two hours' time the antidote will be destroyed—that will be one step in the right direction. Afterwards there'll be a lot of sabotage—you've had a taste of it already; that ought to be warning enough."

He picked up his hat and went out.

Craigie heard him open the front door and go down the stairs, and he heard the street door slam with a hint of finality.

Beneath the smoking debris of Lyddon House, unaware of the strenuous efforts being made to clear the rubble away, Loftus recovered consciousness less than half an hour after the explosion.

The smell of gas prevented him using the lighter which he took from his pocket, but he had a small electric torch, which he took out; its bright beam shone on the caved-in ceiling, the slanting walls and the other four people. All of them seemed unconscious, and a heavy beam was resting on Mike Errol's legs, holding him down.

He switched off the torch and began to get up.

It was difficult, because he had fallen awkwardly and the straps of his artificial leg had come out of position, but he managed to adjust them and then stood up. He had to crouch, for the ceiling immediately above his head sagged dangerously.

Someone called: "Who's that?"

"Loftus," he said, his heart leaping. "Don't try to move, Mike, there's a plank of wood keeping you down."

"I knew there was something," said Mike Errol. "How are you placed?"

"Not badly," said Loftus. "Stay there."

He switched on the torch to see the position of the beam, then stepped gingerly towards Mike and began to lift it. It did not give him half as much trouble as he expected and soon Mike was standing by him and announcing with satisfaction that he also had a torch.

"What about the others?" he asked.

They found that only Julia was hurt; she had an ugly gash in her shoulder, caused by a nail. The others were bruised, but no limbs were broken. Within twenty minutes all of them were conscious and all were coughing, for the slightest movement brought down clouds of dust. They could not move far, but the trapdoor which Grey had used was only lightly covered with debris.

"We can get out," Loftus said.

The floor and sides of the tunnel were slimy, and the fustiness started them coughing again. There was no light except the thin beam of Mike's torch, and he used it sparingly, for they wanted to conserve the batteries in case they came up against another emergency.

It was when the torch was off that Mike stumbled against something on the floor. He recovered himself, switched on the torch, and revealed a pile of earth and stones which reached to the top of the tunnel, completely blocking it.

After a long silence, Grey said:

"Now we're done!"

"How deep is the tunnel?" Loftus asked.

"About ten or twelve feet," said Grey, "and there's solid rock in places; there isn't a chance of getting up without tools." He seemed more affected than the others, although Julia's breathing had quickened.

"What happens if we go in the other direction?"

"It's a dead end," Grey said, "the tunnel finished just about where we came in. Just past this fall it goes in two directions, one to the Guest House grounds, the other to the drive gates." His voice was monotonous; he gave the impression that the discovery had robbed him of all hope. "We might as well go back and wait; I suppose they will try to dig us out."

The return seemed to take much longer; all of them were breathing hard and the coughing fits were more frequent by the time they reached the trapdoor. It showed in the light of the torch which Loftus switched on from time to time.

He said: "We'll go on a bit, I think."

They went on for about ten yards and found the tunnel getting narrower and narrower; there seemed no hope that Grey was wrong. When they reached a point where Loftus could go no further, he switched on the torch again and looked about him. Black earth, dripping with water and slime, was all that he saw—except one little light patch above his head. He leaned forward, grunting with the effort, and touched it.

"Have you made a find?" asked Mike from the rear.

"I wouldn't be surprised," said Loftus in a queer voice. "That feels like cement. What's cement doing as far down as this? It's light, too; if it had been there any length of time it would have become discoloured."

No one responded, but hope flared up again.

"I'm too fat to do anything," said Loftus. "Mike, you're the thinnest one here—see what you can find out."

They had to go back to the trapdoor and Loftus hoisted himself up gingerly, while Mike squeezed past in order to get at the cement. He took out a penknife and got within easy distance of the patch. He scraped the earth about it and found that it dropped away easily, and within ten minutes a patch of comparatively new cement, nearly a yard square, showed in the light of the torch.

"Not bad at all," said Loftus, softly. "I wonder how thick it is?"

"We can hardly dig through it with a penknife," said Grey.

Loftus snapped: "You're quite the Jonah, aren't you?"

Grey grunted, and sounded abashed, and, after an awkward pause, Julia said that she thought there had been some tools in the cellar where they had been trapped.

"That's more like it!" said Loftus.

They unearthed two coal hammers and a small chopper after a wearying search. Grey entered into it with a will, as if ashamed of his earlier attitude, and he volunteered to be the first to use the hammer.

Grey worked hard, and soon they could hear his heavy breathing. Working in that atmosphere and in cramped space was exhausting, and Mike soon took over. Hammond, who had said very little, followed him. Julia wanted to take her turn, but Grey insisted on starting again. At the end of half an hour they had cleared a much wider expanse of concrete, which was apparently part of a wall.

One thing had become obvious.

The earth near the wall had been loosened when the wall had been built in, and it was easily moved. They trampled it underfoot as they worked, one at a time; another hour passed surprisingly quickly.

Hammond was at the wall, clearing the soft earth away, when suddenly he exclaimed and pitched forward.

"Bruce!" exclaimed Mike, who was just behind him. He switched on the torch and saw Hammond's feet, waving wildly in the air; Hammond had fallen through where the soil must have been very thin, and the wall had subsided. After a pause he called out that he was all right, and soon he was facing them through a hole in the soil, and there was excitement in his voice.

"This is big enough for a coal-mine!" he said.

"Now what have we found?" asked Loftus.

All of them went through in Hammond's wake; they found themselves in a wide tunnel, obviously constructed fairly recently. The floor was of earth, but the walls had been packed hard and were shored up with wooden staves. In one direction there was nothing to be seen; the darkness was intense; in the other there was a faint glow of light.

Soon they turned a corner and saw where the light came from.

It was a glass door. They could see the shadows of men on the panel and hear the murmur of voices. The passage led on, and Loftus pulled the others up, seeing something of their dishevelled appearance for the first time.

"Bruce, you and Mike had better go on with Grey and Julia. Make sure you know the way to get back once you get out, and keep your weather eyes open. I expect they've got guards posted."

He waited until they were out of sight, and then approached the door. It was unlocked, a sure indication of how safe the people here considered themselves. The voices were indistinguishable until he opened it a little. Then he heard Hartley's voice.

"In my view, it is fantastic; even if Craigie were disposed to compromise, he won't be able to exert enough influence. Brenn is risking his own safety, and ours with it."

He was answered by Henry, whose voice held an angry note; Henry was incensed at any criticism of his master.

"Mr. Brenn *never* makes mistakes," he said.

"Don't talk nonsense!" snapped Hartley. "It was a mistake to blow the house up."

"It was the only thing to do. If Loftus and the others had got away they would have known all about the way from here to the Guest House. They can't stumble across our system of communications *now* at all events. I shall report to Mr. Brenn when he returns," he added, nastily.

"I've got something to say to Brenn myself," said Hartley.

An uneasy silence followed.

Loftus did not reveal himself, although with the gun in his pocket he would probably have been able to overcome them with the advantage of surprise. He wanted to hear everything that was said, and he hoped that he would be able to stay there until Brenn returned. He might then hear something of vital interest. He was still waiting when he heard heavy footsteps echoing loudly along the passage, and he drew further away from the door. A man came striding along suddenly visible in the light. He walked with a limp. He reached the door and flung it open—*and Loftus recognised Jim Dale!*

After a long pause, Dale said:

"You—damned—fools! They've got out and they must have passed this door. They're bringing dozens of men along the passage. I've closed the partition, but it won't take them half an hour to get that down. We've got to clear out at once!"

Henry snapped: "But Mr. Brenn—"

"He can take his chance," said Dale, savagely, "if he hadn't been so clever it would never have happened. Hartley, collect what papers you want and make sure of those formulae, especially that for the antidote. Henry, collect all the records. McFarlane, set the time fuses; we'll make sure they don't get anything, and with luck they'll go up in smoke this time."

Loftus' lips were curved in a smile as he stepped forward, taking out his gun with his right hand and opening the door wider with his left. They were standing or sitting in chairs in a small room, which was furnished like a lounge, and all were staring at Dale, who had his back to the door.

"On second thoughts," said Loftus, "stay just where you are—including you, Dale!"

He saw Dale stiffen; then the man spun round. The malignance in the face which had always seemed so friendly was a horrid thing. Dale's right hand flew to his pocket, but Loftus fired before he reached his gun.

19

THE TRUTH ABOUT DALE

Dale's hand fell to his side, and he drew back, the colour draining from his face; but he did not fall. Loftus moved towards the wall, near the door. Hartley sat staring, and Mrs. McFarlane was standing erect, her lips parted.

Henry spoke in a curiously soft voice.

"Loftus again. Well, well!"

He was standing by his chair, his face blank, his hands by his side—and then he flung himself forward, ignoring the gun in Loftus's hand. He had a grim look on his face, but it disappeared, and his expression altered completely as Loftus fired and the bullet took him in the chest. He reared up, and his knees bent; slowly he collapsed half-way between Loftus and his chair.

The echo of the second shot was loud in the room.

"Any more for any more?" asked Loftus, inanely. "Don't try to use your little darts or hypos, they won't help you either. Well, well," he added, with a sharper note in his voice, "Mrs. McFarlane, that was in your mind, was it? Put your bag down. *Put it down!*"

The housekeeper had been slowly opening her handbag, which was near her chair, and Loftus had seen her stiffen when he mentioned the darts. For a moment he thought that she would defy him, but Henry began to groan with pain; she withdrew her hand swiftly.

"Throw your bag against the wall," Loftus said, "and don't aim it at me."

She obeyed and then sat down slowly, looking at Hartley. Loftus looked from one to the other, keeping his ears strained to catch any sound. Dale had told him near enough that no one was in the passage between the door and the entrance, and it looked as if the underground chamber was deserted but for that little party.

"I don't think you quite understand," Dale said. "Loftus, listen to me. What we know, what we've discovered, is worth more than a fortune; it's the biggest money-making scheme in history. It will give us absolute control of industry, and there is no need for us to stop at this country. Don't let it be thrown away. You can take a cut, and—"

"Oh, no," said Loftus, "I won't listen to drip of that nature. Didn't anyone ever tell you, Dale, that we're not all interested in making our fortunes, that we don't all want power for its own sake? Whatever you've discovered won't be wasted; it will be used to the greatest good of the greatest number—which is not an original phrase, but it covers my meaning. And, you know, this isn't an unfair world. If you'd handled it legitimately you would have got all you wanted out of it. Some people never learn."

Then he heard footsteps.

There seemed to be a number of people hurrying, and he thought they were coming from the entrance of the tunnel; he did not doubt that Hammond and Mike were returning with reinforcements.

He felt a curious sense of elation.

He believed that Dale would still try to make some last minute move to save himself if nothing else, and he was very watchful. Hartley's silence was a curious thing, and Mrs. McFarlane was now looking towards him as if she wished she could throw the darts with her eyes. The room was very quiet, but the noise of footsteps drew nearer and the tension in the prisoners increased.

Then Loftus saw a shadow on the inner door, which was of glass.

A hand appeared round the door. It seemed to be empty. The opening of the door and the movement of the hand were uncanny, because of the silence. Then Loftus saw that the hand was not empty; between the thumb and forefinger was a tiny object, which he recognised as one of the darts which had already been used so advantageously. He moved swiftly to one side.

He heard the dart strike against the wall.

He could not move swiftly enough for his own satisfaction, but he fired through the glass, and he knew that his bullet reached its mark. Whoever was on the other side exclaimed with pain, and then fell against the door and staggered into the room.

The sight of him nearly put Loftus off his guard, for to all intents and purposes it was Witherspoon, *whom he had seen dead!* He stared towards the man, but recovered himself swiftly enough to see Dale put his hand towards his breastpocket and draw something out. He swivelled his gun round and Dale tossed a wallet to the table. Mrs. McFarlane rushed forward, risking a bullet, and snatched it up. Some papers fell from it, and she selected one.

Hartley flicked a lighter into flame.

It all happened with bewildering speed, first one thing and then another. Loftus, handicapped so much by his artificial leg, could not get near in time to stop them all, and he had only three bullets left in his gun. If they made a concerted rush at him he would not be able to prevent them from doing what they wanted.

Hartley had the lighter burning with a steady flame and Mrs. McFarlane thrust the paper towards it. Loftus realised what was happening and tried to get forward, but Dale ran at him just as he fired at Hartley. The bullet missed, and he lost his balance and fell heavily.

He had no doubt as to what was on that paper: the formula for the antidote. They knew that they had no chance, and intended to destroy everything they could, so as to leave a trail of tragedy and blindness behind them.

He shouted: "Hartley, don't do it! *Julia's blind!*"

The thought flashed into his mind swiftly and he saw Hartley snatch the lighter away. A corner of the paper was already burning and Hartley took it from Mrs. McFarlane and pressed the flames out with his fingers.

"It's not true!" screamed Dale, "destroy it, destroy it!"

But Loftus heard voices from outside and knew that the few seconds' delay had been enough. He rose slowly and leaned against the wall as the door was thrust open and Hammond and Mike appeared at the head of a dozen men.

Loftus knew that it was all over, and his chief thought was of the man who looked like Witherspoon. That went swiftly from his mind, for Hartley spoke above the clamour, his words ringing out:

"Garnett, if you've harmed Julia—"

Loftus stared towards him; even Hammond and Mike drew up. *Garnett.* The name echoed and re-echoed in his mind. *Garnett.* The inventor of the process which had begun much of this business, the man whom Fergus Grey had said had been murdered, and whose death "by accident" had been confirmed. *Garnett.* He looked towards Dale—

In a flash of understanding he knew why Mandino had been murdered.

A large party gathered at the Guest House in the middle of the morning. Dale, Hartley, Henry—who was at death's door—Mrs. McFarlane and the man who looked like Witherspoon, were already in a Black Maria on the way to London, but they had talked freely; most of the mysteries were solved.

That flash of intuition had been vindicated.

Dale was Garnett; and he had been able to listen into all that happened at the Guest House through the wiring-system. During the meeting, when Grey had been interrogated, he had heard

Mandino say to himself: "Garnett, of course!" That had told Dale that Mandino, who had known him as Garnett but had not identified him at the Guest House, had suddenly realised who he really was.

So Dale had gone upstairs and killed the blind man.

"How on earth did you manage to pass him as O.K.?" Mike asked Craigie.

"That was one of the worst features of our part in it," Craigie admitted, "but I don't see that it could have been avoided, although I might have checked even further back than I did. There was a man named Dale, who was badly injured in an air crash, and was invalided out of the R.A.F. His face was badly disfigured. Witherspoon found him and offered to try to make his face more normal, but actually he was murdered. Garnett, who was already one of Witherspoon's patients and quite unrecognisable as his original self, took his place.

"That gave Garnett all the background he wanted. He met Martha and, as far as I can gather, he really fell in love. At all events, the marriage and their decision to take over the house and turn it into a private hotel supported the reports which I had received. The real Dale had lost his money and did need to make an income, and it certainly served Garnett's purpose."

"I still don't see why it mattered all that much whether he were known as Dale or Garnett," Mike said, as they sat in the lounge, very much at their ease.

"Mike has his poor moments," said Hammond, with a grin.

"Once Dale was identified as Garnett it would be known that he was in the racket. He wanted to keep quite outside it. If anything failed he wanted to be in the clear: it was essential for his secret to be preserved. That explains why he allowed Brenn to attack us at the Guest House when Martha was locked in the telephone cupboard. It was calculated to inspire confidence in him and his household."

"H'm," said Mike, abashed. "All right, I'll grant you that, but how did he come to life again?"

Loftus said: "When he failed to get financial support for his idea, at the time it was first invented, we know that he was approached by Brenn. He told Brenn something Grey did not know—that directors of the Mid-Southern knew of the invention and were planning to force him to reveal it. Brenn hit upon the idea of faking his death. What matters is that Garnett was from then on a full partner with Brenn and Witherspoon in an effort to get complete control of the synthetics industry and so apply the invention."

Craigie, who was with them, looked up with a smile.

"People will say, 'It couldn't happen,' Bill. They won't realise that there will always be men who will try to get power into their own hands. Power through huge wealth."

"So, Dale was Garnett," said Mike, "but Fergus Grey knew him, and—"

"You forget the redoubtable Witherspoon," said Loftus. "He was not only an 'eye' man, but a plastic surgeon of no mean ability. Plastic surgery is the answer to disguise—over a long period, it can be done. Even fingerprints can be altered if it's done thoroughly enough. The only snag, of course, is the voice. Dale controlled his. Mandino, according to what Pamela told Christine this morning, knew that Dale's voice was familiar, but could not place it. Presumably, Mandino, whose hearing had become extremely sensitive and who heard us talking to Errol, heard the name Garnett frequently and realised who Dale was. We know what happened after that."

"Only too well," said Mike. "So Mandino really wasn't involved?"

"Mandino's story was true; he had a personal feud with Brenn and Witherspoon, which was why he was blinded. Pamela's story was also true, although it was so remarkable that we were all inclined to doubt it. Brenn tried to head us off towards Mandino when he first saw Mike, and the reason for that is simple, too. He not only wanted to sidetrack us, but he thought Mike might be rescued. He was sure that we would switch over to the Mandino angle, and since Mandino's knowledge was out of date, that would have given him time. Then he was able to take Mike away, and he started the elaborate deception; it very nearly came off."

"Well, now—about Witherspoon?"

"He *was* killed at St. Albans, but, thanks to his plastic surgery accomplishments, he had made what we can call a replica of himself. Mike once overheard him and Brenn talking at St. Albans after he had been moved to a room next to Brenn's study. That move was deliberate; he was intended to hear, and intended to be allowed to escape afterwards. All Henry's searching made it seem to him that they were desperately anxious to get him back. You'll remember that I had had a visit from Witherspoon when he moved to the Guest House. Actually it was the doctor's double who came there; the idea was to confuse us. The double was to take all the knocks, but, as it happened, he survived his maker. The double was a man of Witherspoon's build, and, of course, Witherspoon's genuine appearance was so remarkably like that of a man disguised that it was easy to work the deception. They were up to all the tricks, and used most of them well."

"I'm the man who covered himself in glory," said Mike, with a grimace. "Just what was the Hartley tie-up, Bill?"

"What it seemed to be: he was the economist of the party, but he kept carefully in the background. It was because he knew of the particular advantages of the tunnel connecting the Guest House grounds with his own that the elaborate underground premises were built, and the place at St. Albans was kept so that if things ever became dangerous then they could be 'driven out' and create the impression that they had no headquarters left to work from. Grey was quite right. Hartley's determination to deny him the house was because of the secret."

Afterwards the Department men looked through the underground rooms, finding workshops, experimental laboratories and offices covering a surprising area. The workpeople—many of whom had lived at Chiswick, and others of whom lived not far from Woking—had not been on duty that night, but lists of their names and addresses had been found. So had the details of Garnett's own invention and of the results of researches in man-made materials; experts were already working on them. The formulae for the lotion which caused blindness, as well as the antidote, were not in Faversham's hands, but a small quantity of the antidote had been found. Carruthers had already been treated; he had offered to be the first, to make sure that the stuff worked properly. It would be some days before they knew the result.

Other things had been discovered.

The sabotage at the Mid-Southern factory and those of the two other places had been staged so as to try to exert more influence on the Department, and to stop the investigation. Brenn had men in most of the large undertakings who did his bidding. The extent of his organisation, built up over so long a period, gave them a better idea of how well it would have been put into full operation.

Mike lit a cigarette and spoke slowly.

"I don't think there are many odds and ends, but—just why were Pamela Mandino and Grey so affected when they first saw each other. Did we get the true reason for that?"

"Yes," said Loftus. "Grey knew that Mandino was a bitter enemy of his uncle, and Pamela was affected because, seeing Grey, she knew it would revive all the hatred in her father; she wanted it to die. I'm more sorry for Pamela than anyone, I think—except—"

"Martha Dale," said Bruce Hammond, quietly.

Loftus nodded.

Martha had known nothing of the real use of the Guest House and nothing of her husband's other identity nor of the work he was doing. The discovery had stunned her, but she had kept going and was even now preparing dinner. Yet they were by no means sure how she would go on.

All of them now realised how Carruthers felt about her.

Loftus said: "The solution to her troubles might be Carry; anyhow, we can't do anything more than we've already done. We've got to sit back and wait for the lotion to work. If it does, and I think it will, we can call it one of our better shows, I think."

* * *

The lotion did all that was expected of it.

Within two days Carruthers was beginning to see again, and Craigie and the other victims were already being treated. Within a week all of them were cured, and there was much rejoicing.

Two other things were clarified.

One thing which had puzzled all of them, but which they had not been able to find out, was the way in which the drug was administered. It could be used in an eye-lotion, put on a handkerchief or passed on through the finger-tips, and, in gaseous form, it could be used by spraying. All methods had been used at various times.

Hartley had worked with Brenn for a long time, but towards the end he had threatened to make trouble unless he were given a greater share in the profits. Brenn had not hesitated to make him a victim, and Loftus had been quite right when he had suggested that Hartley had been made blind so as to bring him to heel.

Afterwards there was a delicate situation at the Guest House, where Carruthers stayed on for a while and Fergus Grey and Julia stayed, too—they planned to get married soon and to live near Woking. There was a subdued atmosphere because of Martha, and yet she was the most cheerful of them all. Occasionally Carruthers, revelling in his restored sight, caught a glimpse of her when she did not realise that he was near, and saw the drawn, haggard expression on her face.

He believed he could make it disappear.

It was not too long before the other members of the Department were quite sure that Carruthers would soon be joining the ranks of the married men. That was after Dale, alias Garnett, Hartley, Brenn and Mrs. McFarlane had been tried and hanged, and lesser members of the organisation had been sentenced to long terms of imprisonment.

It was long after the last trace of the plague of blindness was gone that the experts were reporting, in something akin to excitement, that the processes and inventions which Brenn had controlled were far ahead in development. Their exploitation would bring a tremendous increase in prosperity, especially in the under-developed countries.

"Whose affairs seem to be set fair," Loftus said to Gordon Craigie in the office at Whitehall.

"By the way, Pamela Mandino's leaving us next week; she's going to some friends in the West Country. I think there's a young man in the offing. Mike and Mark 'phoned up, while you were out, and asked for a month's leave. I gave them our blessing."

Craigie nodded.

"Bruce telephoned to say that he'll be back next week," added Loftus, "and I've heard rumours from Pip Evans and Reggie Pitt and a few others to the effect that they're getting tired of kicking their heels again. Some people are never satisfied, are they?"

Craigie laughed.

ABOUT THE AUTHOR

John Creasey, born in 1908, was a paramount English crime and science fiction writer who used myriad pseudonyms for more than six hundred novels. He founded the UK Crime Writers' Association in 1953. In 1962, his book *Gideon's Fire* received the Edgar Award for Best Novel from the Mystery Writers of America. Many of the characters featured in Creasey's titles became popular, including George Gideon of Scotland Yard, who was the basis for a subsequent television series and film. Creasey died in Salisbury, UK, in 1973.

DEPARTMENT Z

FROM OPEN ROAD MEDIA

OPEN ROAD

INTEGRATED MEDIA

Find a full list of our authors and
titles at www.openroadmedia.com

FOLLOW US
@OpenRoadMedia

www.ingramcontent.com/pod-product-compliance
Lightning Source LLC
Chambersburg PA
CBHW031102020726
47495CB00007B/2010